D1526915

There's No Such Thing As
ORDINARY WOMEN

by
Teresa Raley

THE
WORDSMITH
PRESS

THE WORDSMITH PRESS

There's No Such Thing As Ordinary Women
by Teresa Raley

Published 2013
The Wordsmith Press
72 Oxford Street
Woodstock
Oxfordshire
OX20 1TX
United Kingdom

ISBN 978-0-9560795-9-6

Cover design by the author
Typeset in New Century Schoolbook
Printed in the USA by
Custom Printing
2001 Cabot Pl.
Oxnard, CA 93030-2666
USA

Dedication

For the ladies in my life without whom
the lights wouldn't shine.

To my parents, who encouraged me to be myself.

To our children, who are making their way
with laughter in their hearts.

To my grandchildren, to whom we pass the baton
with complete faith.

To Lynda, the truest of friends. I would never choose
to go through life without a "Cakes" to keep me in
bounds…or out of them as the occasion dictates.

And, of course, to my husband Devlin, whom I cherish
beyond his imagination.

Contents

Ordinary? Hardly!

Flopped in the never-quite-comfortable Morris chairs on the porch, we laughed and cried our way through the boxes of pictures. God knows we had each vowed to put the pictures in albums one day, but that day hadn't yet arrived. What wonderful stories the albums would tell! But perhaps the randomness of the shoebox method paints a truer picture. Liz tossed a classic shot onto my lap.

There we were. The six of us. Doctor, Lawyer, Indian Chief. And proud owners of a rambling, dilapidated eight bedroom early California ranch house and too much imagination. Maybe we were drawn together by circumstances or by our woman-ness or by our very extraordinary differences, but whatever the glue, it was permanent.

1 Discovery of The House

No one could ever forget the gentle, portly postman who took that picture. His name was Bert, short for Albert. When we asked him to take a picture of us on the porch, he said softly, "I hope you ladies don't expect too much from this here house. The neighbors are right pleased that somebody's willin' to give it a chance." Somehow, his taking that picture made him a co-conspirator in our plans. After that first encounter, he always had a morsel of advice to share when he saw one of us. Sometimes it conveyed his sense of urgency, as in "Better get movin' on that roof 'fore the storm hits this weekend" or his sense of thrift, as in "You ladies certain you need this fancy banister? I can get a pine one for you a lot less" or even his sense of playing within the rules, as in "Don't you ladies have men to do that heavy lifting?" He never did understand that we had perfectly capable men whom we chose not to spend that way. People like Bert don't just happen every day. They are the people who volunteer to coach soccer and never miss a practice. Or the guys who read People Magazine to the residents at the Senior Center. Or the ninety-two-year-old lady who brightens everybody's day by tending the flowers outside her neighbors' windows. There is probably a word to describe such people and if there isn't, there should be.

The House was a great idea fueled in part by our overestimation of our collective talents and available time. The plan was that we would buy a house with great character, structurally sound, but in need of work. We would scrape and sand and paint and hammer and drill until we could proudly introduce The House as a first-class inn featuring elegant themed rooms, five star brunches, idyllic views and picnics worthy of Gourmet mention. It would have at least six full suites: one for each of us. An inn transitioning to assisted living for all of us as needed. We could live together as long as we wanted. It seemed so reasonable that we never dedicated any energy to the details, which may have been a mistake.

Contrary to prevailing myth, we did not seek out that particular house. It found us.

As was our custom a couple of times a year, we were off on a hooligan weekend – just the girls. Husbands didn't necessarily approve of our hen parties, but some things you just have to do. At least the weekends caused less unrest at home than the trips to places like Paris and San Miguel de Allende. So off we went to a glitzy Indian casino and resort to gamble like wild women and see Aretha Franklin in concert. Rachel really would have preferred Asleep At The Wheel, but the quasi-feminists among us opted for a little Respect. Not that anybody cared which star we were seeing; the important thing was our being someplace we'd never been. A little bit of adventure can make up for a whole bunch of tacky. En route we stopped at a chi chi restaurant in an ancient hotel, featuring imaginative (read weird and largely untested) salads and an extensive wine list designed to make the driving more pleasant. I can't help but wonder at what age it becomes okay again to eat rare beef and drink milkshakes. After far too much time spent lingering over mediocre wine, we took our unsatisfied appetites back to Catherine's van, which simply refused to start. We tried everything we knew, mostly looking under the hood into that manly abyss as if it were a sinkhole.

Our collective patience ran out after about ten minutes. Alex decided that she would be better served by going back to the restaurant where she could order profiteroles and watch the drama from an upholstered chair. Rachel, dear Take Charge Rachel, was off like a shot to find an unwitting mechanic she could charm into spending his Friday afternoon rescuing a bunch of old women. It took her just seven minutes to return with a slightly greasy but pleasant-looking young man in tow claiming he could get us back on the road in short order. He introduced himself as James, which matched the name on his shirt but he much preferred Jimmah. Jimmah felt confident that he could have the van fixed in less than an hour. Rachel probably didn't notice that he was obviously more interested in her than in the van, but that's what her figure is for: luring ordinary people into being helpful. Why he heard "breast" when Monica said "blessed" escaped Rachel completely.

Leaving Rachel to continue to hypnotize the mechanic and Alex to eat her profiteroles, the four unoccupied members of the group decided on a short stroll to fill the time. Three and a half blocks later we were standing in front of our dream house, a falling-down two-story lean-to surrounded by foot-high weeds, trash and dead things.

Best of all, it had the magic sign:

For Sale
Foreclosure
Priced for immediate action

I suspect that we looked a lot like Juan Diego when he first saw Guadalupe, and I imagine we felt just about like he did: scared spitless and as excited as an eleven-year-old boy about to launch the first rock with his new slingshot. No boundaries. Cell phones at the ready, we made our first big decision: Liz would place the call to the realtor. She was, after all, a banker of some repute, and the least likely to giggle, swear or experience incontinence in the middle of negotiations. And she didn't have a husband to whom she had to explain the vagaries of this kind of ownership. Liz placed the call to Cyndi, the local realtor with the listing for The Manse. She returned the call immediately and offered to show us The House as soon as she could get there, which turned out to be less than ten minutes. Rachel and Alex had just begun to wonder about our whereabouts when we called them to come check out our fabulous find. Rachel and Alex came post haste in the now-purring van, arriving just as Cyndi pulled up. As we gave Rachel and Alex the abbreviated story, Cyndi collected her papers and joined us. Alex was more than a little perturbed not to have been included in the discovery and unable to understand that it made no difference. We promised that she would be consulted on everything from then on. We lied. On the other hand, Rachel revealed that she had sensed The House when we drove into town and felt a cosmic vibration when she saw it. Of course we said yes. The easiest thing in the world is to say "yes" to Rachel because she responds so enthusiastically with praise for everything you do.

The family that built this stately gabled ranch house obviously had us in mind. It was perfect. Just perfect. Originally built on a ten thousand acre piece of land for raising Cain, cattle and nine children, it was built of adobe gleaned from the ranch and bricks fired by local Indians. The porch was deep and inviting, whispering hints of countless stories to be told. There was a widows' walk on the roof with a pretty picket rail to keep the children from going over the side when they chose to sleep up there to escape the heat of summer.

Cyndi had thoughtfully brought us an old print of the house taken in the twenties and showing a gala Fourth of July party with lots of family and friends. Clearly this family knew how to make "party" a verb. Remembering that the drive from the city to the ranch, even without car trouble, took the better part of a long day, their parties definitely had to be worth attending. In the photograph there are at least thirty people, and there appears to be a suckling pig roasting in the yard. Several guests are raising glasses to some new arrivals in a spectacular Packard touring car. Some of the younger guests are wearing swimming clothes, bespeaking the existence of a natural water source or a pool. Indeed it turned out that there was a swimming pool at one time, but it had long since been filled in. We were fairly certain that we could live without it.

According to Bert, the property was sold in the late

thirties to two likeable brothers who were raised nearby and spoke eloquently about their plans to develop the property without sacrificing the ranch's history. Somehow, they convinced themselves that strip malls at each end of the property would provide services, color and visual definition for the development. Shortly thereafter, the brothers had a bit of conflict when one brother was found to be woo-ing or perhaps woo-woo-wooing his sister-in-law. The result of this liaison was that the attorneys got richer and the brothers split the property right down the middle along the north side of the house. In fact, you could stand on one brother's property line and see the stuffed hawk over the fireplace in the other brother's living room. It didn't look like it had much promise for brothers at odds. A few attempts had been made to bring the ranch back to life, including a brief courtship by the California State Parks or the Department of Fish and Game, but eventually it was sold in civilized, manageable "ranchettes" better suited to croquet than cattle. That is, except the 105 acre piece of property on which the house still stood. And then came The Ladies, as the neighbors called us. Or at least that's what they called us when we first met. We think.

The county's historical society has had enough interest in the house to have maintained a file of photographs, writings, and records, all of which would prove to be valuable in our restoration. But for now, years of neglect stood between us and a full understanding of the size of the task we had undertaken. We did try to navigate the broken porch steps with varying levels of success but all we could really see was the exterior. The good news (and we can always find good news) was that the underpinnings of the wrap-around porch were intact and nearly all of the old wavy glass windows had been removed and stored carefully, or at least fairly carefully. Actually, the previous owner had gone to some costly and mostly futile lengths to preserve his investment, including putting on a new roof and boarding up the windows to keep the weather at bay.

So we just signed papers that Cyndi kept producing over the course of several days until we had half a landfill of documents declaring us the owners of a property we hadn't seen inside. But the escrow papers contained some reassurances such as those promising that plumbing and electricity were just hook-ups away. Just call us the Sight Unseen Sisters, but in this particular case they were right about the plumbing and electricity; we would have to move things around but for the time being we did have lights and running hot but mostly cold water. Because the house lacked some of the basic amenities and didn't "show well," the price was close enough to free that we didn't even pretend to haggle. And dividing any payment by six makes it seem highly manageable. So we agreed to add $5,000 apiece into the kitty in addition to the $3,000 we each started with. Which is just about when it became obvious that we were now getting into real money, which connected to imperatives like retirement. And we knew $48,000 would barely scratch the surface. I suspect that at least one of us fantasized a big win at the casino, but I can assure you that an offsetting jackpot was not to be had.

We thank the previous owner every day, despite the fact that he moved to Oregon the minute our check cleared and maintains a home in the mountains with no telephone, cellular or otherwise. I suppose he really shouldn't have to answer a bunch of silly questions like where is the fuse box? (Even though we knew he tossed it into the trash.) Or who were Becca and Tony, the two young people we had found living on the back porch?

Suddenly, the big bad utilities, which have come to symbolize everything ugly about government, were banging on our non-existent door demanding payment for electricity used by the house since it was last sold. Since the 1930s? I THINK NOT. The change of address you filed with the post office is not your friend. That harmless looking Change of Address card assures you that you will continue to receive all the same advertising literature as well as new stuff for new parents, home improvements and newlyweds. It is the trigger for all kinds of delinquent usage. Sometimes the nice customer relations representative in India will take care of it for you, especially if you are quick to come up with your Social Security number. Uh huh. The local government hasn't a clue. Even the escrow people didn't seem to be concerned as long as we had the "proper legal description." They also suggested that we name our own street and choose a street number.

The first stroll we took in that direction may have been as close to a donnybrook as we have ever had, so we decided to resolve it on a road trip from which nobody could readily escape. That problem put to one side for the moment, we set about beginning our reconstruction. As we focused on the work at hand, Rachel exploded into the library like a hysterical banshee, every fiber of her body engaged in her revelation. "Oh my God, you guys, we haven't got a name!! Just because we haven't paid attention to the big picture and now we have to do things the fast way instead of the right way. For heaven's sake, SOMEbody help me here. THAT'S no way to run a business. We can't have anything printed. I can't believe we dropped THAT ball. Does anybody want a cup of herb tea? Okay. Okay. Let's just figure this out." True to form, Monica chose that moment to breeze through the crisis room as if she couldn't be touched by crisis and Alex, get IN here! I just can't believe it. Alex, do you have any entries for our street names? The long and short of it was pretty simple: "No." Well. If we had to drop a ball, this was an easy one. All of our printed materials would be produced by the upscale printing and specialties company unless we could produce them in-house. That constitutes pull if there ever was any. Rachel had singlehandedly shared her panic and created a focused group of achievers and then turned them into a formless, shapeless bunch of nitwits.

"As a matter of fact, Rachel, before you spontaneously combust, we do have entries and they're not bad," said Monica, passing Liz a sun tea jar with sixty-one entries in it. So we spread our entries out on our poor woebegone card table. We took turns picking up an entry and putting it in boxes hastily labeled YES or NO or MAYBE. No questions asked. After we had given each entry at least a cursory look, we had six remaining choices. And the two winners, by closed ballot, were (do I hear a drum roll?) Lupine Way and Garden Street.

Now, if we could only name The House with as little hassle, we'd be set. We decided to gather at cocktail hour and work until we were all satisfied. This Working to Consensus business could be a hit. That agenda would include music, the curious o-ring, a trip to San Miguel de Allende, dogs, menus, status of individual suites, and anything else that went with rum. First, we carefully calculated the time we'd need to spend on the work doing it ourselves. As we continued to add to the lists, we estimated that, given the fact that we had real lives to attend to, we would be finished in 137 years. Back to the drawing board. We knew that we were capable of restoring the porch (well, maybe not the railing), so we hired the recommended crew from Windows R Us to put the rescued windowpanes back in and replace the missing ones. By the time they were finished replacing the wood, replacing the glass, glazing and caulking, the tab was close to what we had guessed. Times five. But they looked beautiful. They'd better. When the sticker shock from the windows abated a bit, we decided to go back to street names. They're lots easier.

In fact, as we sat down with our cocktails, the first thing Liz said was: "Garden Lane. I like it!" We were all delighted with the decision. We'd barely just taken ownership of this palace, and we had created an address. Such power! But The House itself still had no name. This, you understand, is not a disabling situation. Think of it! Everything you see has a name. Some names are good, some names are not so good. Mostly names are just there. The award for obscure names should go to pharmaceutical companies who, I believe, go into huddles in small structures similar to wigwams, and together add letters to an already existing word until it is unpronounceable by the human tongue, and voilà! A new medication is born.

"Where The House touches the sky," Liz continued, "and the air brings the colors home, the name of the house will be revealed." We all said OK. We'd let The House name itself.

2 Architectural Planning Paper

It seems only logical to anticipate that any group of six women would change addresses, likes and dislikes, spouses, and myriad major and minor elements of their lives with some frequency. It also seems reasonable that the relationships within the group would be fluid, which is not necessarily to say alcohol fueled, though in many situations the addition of a cocktail or two does seem to help. This particular group of women will just barely tolerate change of any kind. The roles are cast in concrete, like it or not, and the rest of the known universe has no say in the matter.

In the formative years, the six of us combined to cover most of the demographic categories. Three of us were married. Three were single. Three had siblings; three were only children. At one time three of us were gainfully employed while three of us were retired. These little factoids serve to validate absolutely nothing, but they make it easier to understand our ever-changing alliances and positions within the group. There was a time when we knew each other's astrological signs, but that stage is blessedly behind us. Not only is it far too difficult to remember Linda Goodman's shared wisdom about sun signs, but it also had to step aside in order to make space for some other wonderment like the degrees of separation between any one of us and our mother-in-law. Face it: when you can't remember your own children's birthdays, it's time to purge the storage systems, which is very hard to do. I, of course, have theories on the subject, one of which is that our brain is much like a room full of file cabinets. The brighter you are, the more quickly your ultra-observant mind fills the file cabinets, leaving us with ever-diminishing storage space and no external storage locker to dump stuff into. That's why smart people become forgetful younger than others. In other cases, you understand, it's simply because the people don't care enough to absorb what others are saying.

A good percentage of our time together, especially in the early years, was occupied by self-discovery exercises that amused pretty much everybody.

On many occasions, each of us brought a query to a group gathering. It was intended to be thought-provoking and revealing, but it may have been just a primitive form of Truth Or Dare. Which is not to say we didn't learn from it. On the contrary, we often learned more than we wanted or needed to know. Such a simple question as, "What is your favorite season?" could open the floodgates of emotional memories, and questions of an entirely personal nature like "Where would you go if you ran away from home?" might draw dead silence or stories of wild encounters, most likely completely fictional or at least modified for plausibility. Or you ask an easy one like, "What is the most memorable outfit you've ever worn?" and the answers pour out. Alex wore a royal blue dress with a sweetheart neckline; Catherine wore a Fifth Dimension outfit and Rachel wore chocolate brown thigh high boots and a blouse with "pouffy" sleeves. And everybody remembers.

Another question is a perpetual entry in a category

covering the most basic relationship challenges. "What trait would you absolutely require in a man you were going to live with?" Although the real answer is without a doubt something filmy like trust, I like the whole concept of "if it feels good, do it." So I would opt for a mandatory trait like the ability to select accurately what's going to feel good from one time to another. Liz said she would hold out for a man who could cry and admit to throwing up.

In one such exercise, we were to ponder the question: "If you could excel at something for one hour, what would you be or do?" There's always a goody-two-shoes who thinks she will save the planet and its inhabitants, but you know perfectly well that she would actually lock her sister away along with her sister's paunchy, perpetually suggestive husband and party until the last dog died. Save the planet? I think no way. Then, on the other hand, there's Rachel, the would-be seductive classical flamenco dancer among us, who declares that she would promptly gather up her favorite men and dance for them. We all know that, in fact, she would do something generous and kind for someone she's never met and then hurry home to her husband, the only man she's ever been with. Alex would be attended to by a coterie of up and coming artists, and possibly a musician or two, each hoping she would give him or her the nod as a patron. She claims that she wouldn't be too demanding of youthful sexual powers, but she would require F&F (frequency and finesse). I would choose to be a torch singer with a seductive whiskey tenor voice performing in a smoke-filled bar where patrons came to drink themselves into love, or at least something close to it. I'd have a stinger at my fingertips and a piano player who knew exactly when it was time for him to escort an amorous fan to the door. Needless to say, I can't carry a tune no matter how large the bucket, and I've never been accompanied by a piano, but the exercise, like everything we touched, made its mark on The House. Where do we put the baby grand piano? Does it go in the living room or the library? It goes in the living room, of course. Otherwise, no one would be able to read or just sit quietly. As if we had a piano to begin with. But, aaahhh, perhaps we do.

Catherine, to no one's surprise, reminded us that her son and daughter-in-law had just replaced their antique but beautiful sounding piano with a brand new one and might give or sell us the "old" one. By the time the conversation had taken another turn, we were so enamored of the new acquisition that we had completely forgotten that our benefactors knew nothing about their generous gift. We enthusiastically renewed our subscription to Only Child Journal and made a note to double up the insulation in the new library walls.

The bigger question should have been "Where is the library?" That seemed simple enough to three of us: Liz, Catherine and me. It would be the large room to the right of the entry. Alex, on the other hand, thought that room would be a perfect place to hold art classes. Rachel saw it as a boutique selling health supplements, sachets, postcards, loose-fitting clothing made from renewable resources like hemp and

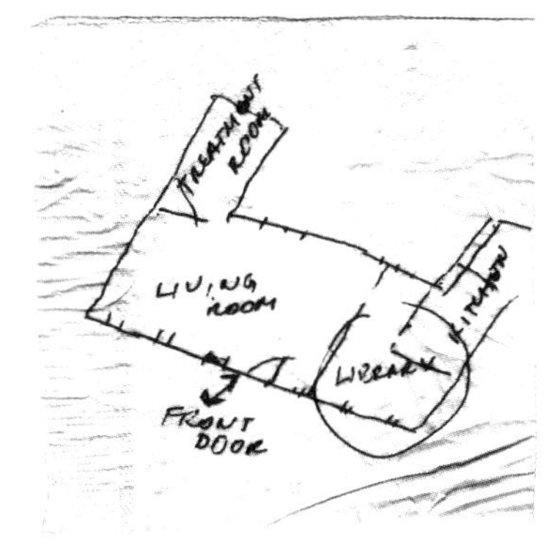

beech. Monica, usually amenable to most ideas, firmly insisted that whatever we do with that room, we must sell local wines. And out came the fast food paper napkins we used for architectural planning because not one of us could remember to bring pad and pencil. So. Now we get to play house again.

As you face The House, the door marks the center of the front wall, an impressive sixty foot expanse punctuated by windows two feet wide and six feet tall. The front door opens into the living room. To the right of the door is the room we called the library until we were proven wrong and it became a dining room in the blink of an eye. A third fairly large room behind the living room was where we planned to put the new staircase. The discussion that ensued was certainly a lesson in communication and an exercise in compromise. Mostly it was a good discussion because the right side won. Now that we had our library/dining room in place, we could start to amass stuff to recycle instead of throwing away. Imagine the recyclables the six of us could generate with catalogues, magazines, coupons, paint chips, paperback books, old newspapers and various other kinds of literary detritus. Obviously, rules would have to be set. Like it or not.

Once we had semi-safe access to the inside of The House, we found our plans and preparations to be inadequate. Not really bad but not great. The House had a lovely, formal, rather funereal salon that would make you remember the word antimacassars without knowing why. We wanted a real living room where a guest could read, play the piano, ponder over a jigsaw puzzle, sip (or slug) a cocktail, or assume a mysterious pose and let 'em wonder. Clearly, the original $30,000 we had earmarked for general restoration would perhaps cover the downstairs or maybe a portion of the eight bathrooms that were a very high priority. No matter. We were crazy about The House. Little things like the twelve inch mahogany baseboards or the century-old brass chandeliers downstairs offset quite a lot of the less lovely aspects of our purchase. The walls, mostly tongue and groove, were in good shape, needing only heroic sanding and paint or finish. The floors were in remarkably good condition. Hope was our general contractor, assisted by her evil cousin, Blind Faith. According to plan, we drew for suites with no whining or notable disagreement. Each of us had the freedom to establish a theme for our suite and decorate it to a fare thee well. It would undoubtedly be hard to let inn guests stay in our very personal quarters, but that's just the way it was. Besides which, we had decided that family treasures could be kept in our personal lockers and not be used for guests.

Common areas we would do together with a unifying theme and within a pre-ordained budget. That's b-u-d-g-e-t for those of us unfamiliar with the concept. Look it up. Now, we all know that budget is a dirty word but sometimes real life simply demands it. And sometimes it's harder to achieve than others.

It didn't really occur to us that the instant we had doors and windows we'd have people, good and not-so-good. We had become fairly well acquainted with Becca and Tony, the couple of young neo-vagrants who had taken up residence in the covered patio in the back and made it their business to know everything happening at The House. It was actually a mutually beneficial relationship, but unless they could prove to be our offspring, we had to refine the relationship a bit. Seems Becca and Tony met on a Greyhound bus between Truckee and Porterville. They had no aspirations to marry and/or propagate. They enjoyed having the freedom to be wherever they were, whenever they got there, and they were evidently making a fairly passable living at this rudimentary property management gig. We sent our negotiating team, Liz and Rachel, to either evict them or hire them. They took it all in stride, thanked us for the free lodging and offered to keep an eye on the place for us. Well, on further reflection, why not? They were youngish, polite, and available for house-sitting. They also had a cellular phone. We extracted several promises from them, including using the Andy Gump rather than the yard and no campfires, just the built-in barbecue. And no guests. It may have been a bit unorthodox, but it seemed to work. Windows done, entry doors ordered, we measured for porch lumber and had it delivered. We were off and running.

Who would have guessed that just a few years later we would be standing on that same porch wearing what we generously called "bridesmaids' dresses."

They were actually costumes mandated by the bride, our dear Monica, who traveled through the 60s letting just enough of it stick to her to make her appear to be a perpetual – if refined – hippie. And it was true – she knew about health foods before Adele Davis took the rest of us to task and felt comfortable talking about things that made debutante Catherine turn scarlet and laugh until she began to snort.

The bridesmaids were to wear gauze peasant blouses with some kind of neutral skirt or pants. We even went shopping together to find matching blouses but of course couldn't reach consensus. We had not enough guidance to make us look quite deliberate, not enough budget to make us look tacky-chic, and not enough good sense to tell the bride to come up with another plan. Nope. So we wore these peculiar post-60s outfits with widely varying fashion success. As the photos commemorate, Liz played by the rules and looked perfectly fine, much as you would expect from a Michigan girl gone west. Alex rebelled against wearing an outfit that would make her appear heavier than "fluffy," and marched herself down to Macy's, against all the rules, where she found something expensive and flattering in a lovely peach color. Typical only child. Catherine, who is a tall, sinewy gift to clothing, looked a lot like a sandhill crane, only with less color. Her western boots were a nice if incongruous touch and her flowing skirt set her apart. Certain that it would someday be needed for a costume, I had saved the genuine article blouse from 1967 when I made it, but nowhere could I find a roach clip to hang from a beaded chain. And then there was Rachel, who always looks like impending sex, regardless of the occasion, and who for the first and probably only time in her life looked pretty close to awful. The crowning touch, as you might have guessed, was the flower garland each of us wore in our hair. Or perhaps the essence of the occasion was Catherine's mother, Charlene, passing out single daisies to the guests from a ribbon-festooned basket. Whatever the individual snapshot that brought a moment back to life, the whole wedding was like a tiny, sacred eruption of an era largely gone from view.

Clearly, this fashion show was in Monica's honor, representing our solidarity in celebrating her capture and domestication of a rare American affluent widower. She and Catherine had used every one of their combined wiles to trap and seduce this character right out from under the noses of a carnivorous gang of grass and sod widows anxiously awaiting his availability. They blinked...just as Monica and Catherine closed in for the capture. And the rest, as they say, is history.

3 The Skill of Innocence

Admittedly, we had some dramatic challenges awaiting our abilities in bringing The House from shambles to shining. We did know most certainly that we couldn't start with Southern California Celebrity Living and end up with two nickels to rub together. Then Rachel, who knows no bounds, comes in for a landing with a suggestion that we make a list of tasks that could be done by unskilled labor, take it to the high school football coach and offer to pay his ballplayers twice minimum wage. Half of the money would go to the students and half would go to the football program. Brilliant! That would get the work done faster and cheaper, make the community know we're good guys, and give something back to this town where we planned to spend a considerable amount of time. She called on the football coach, who loved the idea and passed it on to the vice-principal, who presented it at a staff meeting and before we knew it, the house was full of scantily clad hard-bodies from both boys' and girls' sports, competing for awards. Ultimately, we even had the Debate Club among our laborers. We served lots of lemonade and watched the decades of paint and varnish turn to dust. Thank you, Rachel! When the school called a special assembly for Rachel to present the first check for $850, she was surprised at the celebrity status she had attained. But Rachel is like that: she really believes that if she had waited ten minutes, somebody else would have had the same idea. Not the least bit self-effacing, rather it's just that she thinks so highly of the rest of the world. And they presented her with a football jersey, which she wears like a giant badge of honor. Show off.

The next thought had to be: "Where do we go from here?" First, we determined that the things we wanted to do would require far more than a Dremel™ could deliver. Much as I love my cordless wondertool, it was going to need some help on this project. As luck would have it, the nearest Big Box hardware store was less than fifteen minutes from The House. Oh wow.

We utilized the Skill Of Innocence, essential to hardware shopping; it is, without a doubt, really an art form, and your level of success is largely controlled by how well you meet the expectations of the store personnel, not your own skill level. I learned it from a Texas lady who explained it like this: "Before you get to the stoah," she said in her perfectly innocent drawl, "mayk a good list and a basic picture of what it is you wont to accomplish. When y'all get there, find you one of those helpful boys in the orange aprons and look him in the eyes as if you think he's a genius. He'll say something pithy like, 'Can I help you find anything, ma'am?'" How can they possibly not know that being called ma'am, even in the South where they've made it a title of distinction, causes an immediate electric shock in a woman's brain that makes her want to strike the offending person? In this case, respond by giving him the list and the rudimentary sketch of what you want and say, "Ah do believe you can." The paper becomes a symbol of his ownership of the project and he will take the initiative to make it work, come hell or high water. DO NOT let him give it back to you. I can feel the feminists out there sharpening the guillotines, but I say use what you have. We have Rachel. When he has completed the revisions to the list and re-done the sketch so that nearly anyone could do it, take the list and plans and study them one last time. Ask if everything you need is on the list and in the basket. Exhausted, he will look it over once again and assure you that you're ready to roll. You can trust him on this because the last thing he wants to see are you and yours coming back in that door with a half-completed project.

For the inaugural hardware shopping trip, we felt it fair that we all go in order to minimize the second guessing that was bound to follow. We made a detailed list with the help of a favorite book, The Guide to Everything Sold in Hardware Stores. As planned, we purchased a circular saw, two hammers, a cordless drill, two handsaws, a hacksaw, a set of screwdrivers, wood glue, gloves, four flashlights, four metal tape measures, pliers, extension cords, a contractor's box of sandpaper, and assorted nails and screws. We hadn't decided whether to rent or buy a commercial sander. As we approached the cashier, having thrown up our hands in frustration at the inconvenience of the self-checkout designed and promoted solely to make normal adults appear to be helpless idiots, it became obvious that one or several of us made independent decisions throughout the store. Among the items added surreptitiously to our three-cart parade were a package of popsicle sticks, no doubt added by Alex with some art form in mind; a set of four fancy wine coasters ("Surely y'all don't expect to do without the basics just because we have a job to do."); and a package of six lint rollers ("Mah lord, ladies, ah do expect that we'll be entertaining in the neah future and we cain't have our guests sit on dusty chairs.")

We all suspected Rachel and Liz were responsible for the six Sunset How-To books, and just possibly the How To Look Past A Plumber's Butt When Selecting A Contractor and maybe even the beefcake calendar featuring twelve months of great pecs and washboard abs. I have no idea who selected the doorbell that plays forty-nine different selections including Be Kind to Your Web-Footed Friend and It's A Small World After All. These are dangerous times. I figured I could always bring my tools from home, which turned out to be a miserable idea because then they are never where you need them.

One thing we absolutely did not want to be was a design review committee, bound and determined to choke off any pleasing idea in favor of attention to historical detail. In fact, one of the first things we asked Cyndi was whether or not we could expect the preservationists to get involved with The House. She assured us that we would not be obligated to please anybody but ourselves. We agreed that if one of us got a bit spiny, we would call for Miss Elizabeth, our mythical behavior monitor, to direct us to a solution.

Catherine is one of those people who really do toss their pashmina wrap over the back of a chair where it resides artfully until such time as it is needed elsewhere. Inspired decorating comes easily to her, so she couldn't wait to get to work on her suite. Some of us harbored visions of Catherine atop a ladder supervising the removal of walls she didn't think we'd need, so Liz extracted a promise that she would not remove walls or cause walls to be removed without consensus. After all, any of us could attest to the fact that the "rip it down, sort it out and start over" approach worked beautifully for her current home, which has been featured several times in regional magazines. There was also some consternation about turning her loose to design her suite because budget is not her strong suit. But decorating certainly is, and she promised to work "within reason." I've never felt that "within reason" was synonymous with "within budget," but I figured somebody braver than I could monitor her expenditure. Liz. There, that's done. Liz would oversee budget and expenditure.

We practically had to hog tie Catherine to get her to help complete the porch and the front steps. The entire time, she was fooling with color chips from one accent color to another and "blah blah blah blah blah" until we could barely listen to another sentence. Finally, Rachel said something uncharacteristic like, "Is anyone tired of Catherine's room yet?" Too close to the truth? Whereupon Catherine went into a brief pout which ended with her hand on her left hip, her right hip thrown out and forward and one arm flailing in description of Catherine's Suite Plan 1. She declared that nobody would EVER be bored with her room. "And," she added with more than a hint of proprietary challenge, "ah intend to call mah suite the Orange Blossom Suite." Funny how that drawl sneaks to the surface in times of crisis. We had long since learned that this product of Dallas' Lofty Class is impossible to argue with. She has combined all of the social skills learned at Cotillion with the combat skills she learned in pursuit of her husband, and voila! She can browbeat anyone into submission with a withering look and that hip thing.

Catherine absolutely adores her husband. Even after forty years, three children, a busload of grandchildren all headed for greatness, and living in more than eighteen cities to stay at the top of his broadcast career, she adores him. Consequently, being away from him for the forty-eight hours it takes to make a work weekend at The House viable is not her choice. She would rather be with him in Timbuktu than without him anywhere. Therefore, in Catherine fashion, she offered to rent a two-bedroom apartment for us to share, as long as she and her husband had first call on one room if they were coming up. Unfortunately, nothing available met her standards. This caused Catherine to hit the unattractive frenzy stage, working like a dervish, barking orders, moving tools and generally being hysterical, knowing that when the Orange Blossom Suite had a bed and bathroom facilities, she and Frank could spend as much time there as they wanted. We just wondered how they'd get along with Becca and Tony, the homeless kids living in the patio of The House. They would all most likely behave as though they were from different planets, but chances were even that Alex would discover something no one had suspected about them, like Becca had tremendous talent with watercolors or Tony's sense of rhythm mandated that he get outfitted with appropriate percussion instruments. Alex would take it from there. She is compelled to make people better than they had any intention of being, whether they like it or not. As for me, I'm just scared of that hip thing.

Rachel isn't the least bit intimidated by Catherine, or for that matter, anyone else as far as I can tell. That could be the result of growing up in a remote lumber camp where relationships were straight out of really, really bad movies. It certainly prepared her for taking on the world. She reminds us of an old story about a salesman who didn't deliver by deadline and was therefore summarily tossed out of the office and told never to return. Every couple of weeks, the salesman called on his former client and received the same rejection. Finally, the client was so tired of the salesman's unwelcome visits that he allowed his secretary to send him in. He asked the salesman why he continued to call on him, and he responded, "How am I going to know if you're still mad?" And their relationship was restored. That would be Rachel. Only then Rachel would have given him some magic potion from her health food kit bag and assured him that it would control his moodiness. And he, under her spell, would believe her completely. In fact, Rachel is much like a human pyramid scheme, the kind of scam that depends on the confidence the victim has for the guy at the top. If Rachel could bottle her magnetism, she wouldn't need to work, but that's how Rachel is. The most evident soft spot she has is for her grandchildren, who will no doubt emulate her sense of purpose just as her daughters have. This becomes a bit awkward when Rachel goes on a new campaign, whether for yam cream or fiber or sandals with separated toes for healthy feet. Her enthusiasm for her discoveries is such that she might pop up as a carnival barker selling kegel weights to the unenlightened at some county fair. Sometimes the solutions overlap prior golden knowledge, but we just accept such conflicts. We do get to an age at which we hope someone will bring up the subject of health, thereby opening the door for soliciting lay advice about the dozens of ailments that sneak up on us. We're too embarrassed to ask our family practitioner about such nagging problems as frequent gas, night drooling, or hair loss not on the head, and Rachel will have just read an article about every subject we bring to the table. She is often right. In addition to her metaphysical self, Rachel is compelled to participate in any and all conversations going on within earshot. She will admit to anyone that she and her family are "The Loud People," and she will advise perfect strangers that they probably don't want to sit at any table they've chosen close by because she and her party will disturb them, regardless of her good intentions.

Rachel is also the one not to sit next to when taking pictures. In the first place, she leads with those magnificent boobs and follows with a toss of the hair and a laughter-provoking smile, which just simply sucks the color out of everyone else. Then she fluffs her hair, which is cut in the shaggy, fresh-out-of-the-sack style, and clips it on top of her head. But for her sense of style she could look like Bam Bam of Flintstone fame. Then she spends the rest of her day securing her hair and re-securing it to the top of her head to no apparent effect.

4 Salt or No Salt?

Although most of our "free" time was spent at The House, working harder than we knew we could, occasionally we would escape from the heat and the intense level of industry at The House and take a jaunt like in the old days to parts unknown. Every now and then one of us would propose taking a guest along. No matter how we tried, we just couldn't find anyone who would be able to keep up or not feel as though they'd been thrown into a tank full of piranhas.

Walking into a gathering of these women already in progress is always much like I would imagine a freefall from a suspension bridge. You just keep falling, mostly because you have no choice. It is not possible to just glance into the room and withdraw. Nope. When you're there, you're there. At a recent weekend gathering, all six of us were in attendance at the perfectly dreadful beach house we'd rented sight unseen, preparing to go into town for a little shopping, a little wine tasting and a little eating. Rachel (who else?) explodes into the room loaded with energy, despite having stayed up until 1:30am. She's wearing a sharp new outfit and doesn't even have time to blink before Liz calls a camel toe on her. Rachel, genuinely surprised at the call, asks me if it's true and I agree with Liz. Catherine adds her agreement and tells Rachel that she should change slacks and get moving. Monica watches the drama unfold as Alex innocently comes into the kitchen only to be braced by a still disbelieving Rachel. Alex isn't exactly sure what a camel toe is, so she votes with the crowd. Rachel gives it up, hikes up the front of her slacks and parades an exaggerated camel toe, all the while threatening to have a camel toe showing while we shop.

Throughout the weekend all conversations were peppered with references to a hot new book someone brought about the ways we can stay looking youthful and sexy, regardless of age. Real issues. Life-changing issues. What color lipstick to wear at what age. What bling to wear and whether to wear bling on your ass. What color denim is appropriate and what cut. What eye shadow, for heaven's sake. Anybody who's still worried about eye shadow has either had her eyes done or hasn't discovered that within minutes of application the color has all scurried up into the eyelid crack never to be seen again. If we're going to take on the subject of making ourselves more beautiful for the sole purpose of catching or keeping a man, then we must address the flip side: what men need to do in order to maintain their tentative attractiveness to women. Women think nothing of enlisting the help of a cadre of plastic surgeons to take a tuck here, a nip here, buffing there and restoring around there. Admittedly, many men seem to age more gracefully than their counterparts, but there are plenty of them who go to seed hardly even noticing it. But it is safe to assume that some of these gentlemen could use a little Testi Tuck to bring them back to their firm youthful self. Just a thought. At least it would be a nice gesture.

From bawdy to beautiful, these women can take control whenever the occasion calls for it. On the clothes shopping portion of this excursion, Liz and I were assigned to "shop" the west side of the street while the four GotRocks shopped the tony east side, finding pants for a mere $190 and cute little camisoles for less than $150 each. Can you imagine such bargains? Seated in yet another contemporary California cuisine restaurant featuring leafy green inedibles and luncheon size (read "miniscule") portions, we played Show and Tell with our newest purchases. We had contributed a little more than sixteen hundred dollars to the local economy. It seemed to me that such a contribution, easily visible in its store-specific shopping bags, would telegraph our importance to everyone. Not so. In fact, it took precisely forty-five minutes to get a grilled cheese sandwich, which of course by then was cold. The server, who clearly had no idea of our importance, did come over promptly to take drink orders and sold three margaritas. When she asked the requisite "salt or no salt" question, Rachel took a break from her facial exercises and asked, with a completely straight face, "Do you have Himalayan Crystal Salt?" The obliging server responded that they had pink, white and black, but allowed as how they weren't yet using it to rim margaritas. And I'm thinking, "Is there a sea in the Himalayas? How come Himalayan salt?" Where on earth, or not on earth, had we gone? We had landed in a zone understood only by people who smoke lavender. It is quintessential Rachel, and I promise to do everything in my power to incorporate that onto her headstone when the time comes. Rachel and Himalayan Crystal Salt. A flawless match.

Alex is the perfect front-woman for any kind of shopping. She admits to being fluffy, which is a very Alex word for overweight, but she always manages to look like a million bucks. She can talk intelligently about many subjects, and she can look convincingly as if there is-not-never-was-never-will-be anyone at home in that blonde head. She is also the paragon only child. Blending the characteristics she has developed, you have a flashy dresser who is absolutely certain that she is entitled to have anything she wants and to reject anything she doesn't want, including Christmas gifts. "I really don't care for this. It's not my style" is as likely as "Thank you sooooo much." With Alex, you almost always know where she stands on any subject, like it or not. Send her in to a VSOP (Very Special and Over-Priced) boutique and she will have the help attending to her – and her friends – like royalty. I think she has earned the title of Duchess. Not that Duchess is the be-all and end-all, but it would facilitate introductions and invitations, allow a certain amount of latitude when it comes to quirky behavior, and look good on stationery.

Actually, Alex is a collage of mostly connected images. A respected patron of the arts and an accomplished artist herself, she has earned a living coordinating art shows and musical events in cities not necessarily prone to supporting the arts. Much of her effectiveness in this arena is due, again, to her firm belief that everyone wants what she wants. She strikes like an owl under the cover of darkness, finding vulnerable decision makers and likely support staff just by asking "Who? Who? Who?" Then by morning, when they emerge into the harsh light of the real world and discover that they have committed to far more than intended, it's too late.

Alex was widowed young and raised her only child, a son, in a world of creativity and travel, a world populated mostly by adults. As a result, he is very comfortable with the generation ahead of his, and he travels like an old pro. A perfect arrangement for both of them: she had an attentive and protective young man to attend to her, and he had a ticket to the world. Now that Douglas is married and has a son of his own, Alex has begun the next round, which promises to be even better because in this incarnation Alex really is Auntie Mame, loaded to the gills and on a hunt and gets better at it by the day. And true to her destiny, this Bakersfield debutante still carries her matched set of white Samsonite luggage, including the make-up

kit, even on jaunts with the ladies. And she's still from Bakersfield. If you should need to be able to describe Alex in ten words or less, you'd say, "She's from Bakersfield and still carries her matched white Samsonite." By way of explanation, she told us that, statistically, the chances of her luggage running afoul of the security people at the airport are smaller than any luggage the rest of us are carrying by seventy-five per cent. I can't imagine why, but the way she explained it made it perfectly plausible. Then and only then, having taken heat about her luggage for years, did she tell us that her in-laws, Hank and Barbara, whom she adored, had given it to her for high school graduation, which made it more valuable to Alex than the sizeable estate they left her. Well, could we possibly have felt any meaner or less well informed? Of course, it made us more observant at airports.

Her Samsonite notwithstanding, she did break down and buy a duffle bag specifically for trips to The House. As you might imagine, it has all the trappings needed by the duchess. It is canvas and leather and has a compartment for everything, probably even eye shadow. Most important of all, it carries the JW Hulme logo, surpassing anything put out by the more commonly seen producers of status-endowing goods. Of course it weighs close to a ton, but that's why God made porters. It's a shame that her affluence waited so long to arrive, but she's doing a fine job of liberating it.

Interesting how varied the paths to money are among this group. Rachel worked for hers, beginning with a stint as a rest home owner and concluding as the premier special projects creator in the county. Alex inherited hers. Liz worked her tail off for a major player in the banking industry, bringing her success to the bank and vice versa. Paid nicely but not equitably. Catherine was born with hers, invested wisely, married the right man (the second time), and continues to watch it grow. Monica spent most of her life living modestly but with adventures the biggest spenders couldn't begin to dream of. In the world of information and news, there is an adrenaline rush around every corner, and she is sharp enough, even in her eighties, to command respect from her peers. With retirement age looming, she fell into a bucket of money, identifying, meeting, and marrying a rare rich American sod widower. He is very nice looking and has a genteel and genuine sense of humor. He actually enjoys travel. They would be an excellent Celebrex couple, but I suspect he would pass on being the national Viagra poster spokescouple. She merged into the lifestyle without a twitch and rarely looks back from her vineyard in the valley. I married an extremely talented artist and graphic designer. Need I say more?

5 Scotty and His Hard-Body Crew

Meanwhile, back at the ranch.

The time we spent together at The House was very rich. There was more laughter than The House could contain. Consequently, it spilled out to the surrounding area with the kind of contagion that builds reputations. When our student labor force was working, they made it very clear that they had a vested interest in both the building and its position in the community. When the sanding of two adjacent walls had almost reached the corner, all fourteen kids who were working that day did an abbreviated cheer and tackled it together. Later, one of the students told me, "That was an important corner – the first one downstairs – and we wanted to own it together. Not just one of us should claim the corner." And back to sanding they went.

Fathers are an interesting subset of adult males, and even more interesting when they become Fathers of High School Football Players. They attain the ability to identify the individuals on two teams of young males from a distance, and believe that they can communicate information to them telepathically. Their pride in these sons is tangible and more than a little frightening when you realize that this pride frees these sires of football studs to use words like "hooters" with impunity. But let that same son get a leadership job, and a paying one at that, and the status points don't transfer to home. The "hail fellow well met" who gives his son a giant public man hug when he comes off the field basks in the afterglow for approximately ten minutes, beyond which Bubba can't hear a word his Boy Bubba says. No audience, no backslaps. Furthermore, packaging becomes critical in dealing with Fathers of High School Football Players. If Boy Bubba wants to use the good car, he needs to be escorting a very attractive girl with a sterling reputation she doesn't deserve. When asking for a favor, send Rachel. We had gently asked if we could borrow sanders, for their own offspring for heaven's sake, but our gentle plea fell on deaf ears until Rachel made one of her assembly visits to the school. No fewer than four of the fathers offered to loan their sons sanders from home. It was a huge boon to the project, but it obviously made a difference when the plea came from Rachel.

The installation of eight bathrooms, or even one if the truth were told, was simply a task beyond our skills so we got in touch with Cyndi, who had a decorator friend who would coordinate the bathroom project for us within our budget. We enthusiastically agreed to meet with her. Rule #1: If you can't stand to look at your decorator, you need to show him or her the door and usher him or her out. It won't work, no matter how hard you try. Being fairly new at this game and coming from a mentoring business society, we believed that we could overlook the lime green hair, the spandex skirt band not concealing blue-white fleshy thighs and the lace blouse with crucifixes barely covering where nipples might be. We met with her three times before her fantasies of a career in Hollywood pushed us past our limit. We did learn that this valley is loaded with failed set designers who have taken on second jobs as trophy wives in training. (That would be Trophy Wives In Training.)

Back we went to the Big Box hardware store to find someone to tackle our bathrooms. Having paid close attention to our early lessons about shopping the Big Box, we were armed with sketches of the bathrooms and where we thought plumbing might go. First, you wait in a customer service line with people who are spending tens of thousands of dollars on kitchen remodels. They sound much smarter than you feel, but they get shuffled off to the kitchen planning section just like everybody else. There is reason to believe that it's all a ploy to keep you from finding the complaint department. When you have waited a sufficient amount of time to earn your Patience Badge, you get to talk to a real person who sends you back to the waiting area by the carpet samples to call someone who has a list of authorized handymen to do the bathroom job. When they finally understood the concept of eight, as in eight luxurious bathrooms in one house, we became very, very important. They reached one of their stable of allegedly competent handymen by phone and made an appointment for him to meet us at The House. So there we stood with our sketches and information, only to be sent home. Apparently, we hadn't learned all the lessons after all. As it turned out, Scotty was very capable, if a little rough around the edges. He used several subcontractors, and managed them masterfully. In our first meeting with him, I suggested that he hire subs according first to their abilities to get the job done within budget and secondly according to their physiques. After all, if some stranger is going to wake you with his or her power tools every morning, you are more disposed to forgive him or her if he or she pleases the eye. For the most part, he followed that suggestion and when he didn't, we offered to let the students finish the job.

Putting our confidence in Scotty and his hard-body crew to create eight gorgeous bathrooms simultaneously was actually bordering on brilliant. Just like a production line except that you get a basin instead of a car. The plumbing is basically the same. Each of us selected a combination shower and tub and we each selected a double vanity and cabinetry from a single manufacturer, increasing the chance that they'd be tooled the same. Scotty contacted the right subcontractors about installation. Otherwise we might spend our later years with bathroom water and no place to put it. Overall, the planning for the bathrooms was straightforward and the choices were remarkably wide. There was no reason that one bathroom would remind anyone of another just because they came from the same supplier. I think my favorite may be the one with the cobblestone floor and seat. Or perhaps the elegant mahogany Williamsburg look.

Those issues resolved, we set about planning the refurbishments for the downstairs. The House is actually U-shaped. Not including the porch, the house is sixty feet wide and sixty feet deep, surrounding a patio with a wonderful barbecue built in the thirties of native stone. Becca and Tony had maintained the patio, or at least had done no damage. They did, however, suspect that their residency was coming to an end, so they did what anyone should under the circumstances: they applied for jobs at The House. Monica, who had become Personnel & Customer Relations by default, saw instantly that they were excellent raw material and started their training long before there was anything to do. She allowed them to stay in the patio while the construction was going on. And Rachel, like a hawk, swooped them up and put them to work on the landscaping, a dress-up word for pulling weeds and moving rocks.

We were generally there on weekends, but as the kids stripped and sanded the walls, ceilings and floors to a fare-thee-well, the light at the end of the tunnel was strong enough to lure us to the property more often and for longer periods of time. Catherine's suite, The Orange Blossom Suite, was coming together very nicely, and as far as we could tell, within budget. The crown molding had a sort of bas relief of vines and branches with an occasional small, round fruit that could only be an orange. She had it hand painted by a local artisan who makes a living adding googaw to otherwise sufficient rooms and pieces of furniture. Fortunately, Catherine was firm in her vision and didn't give the artiste, LucyAnne, free rein. Each of us had begun to oh so tentatively plan the details of our own suites. Liz's suite was to be called first The Hummingbird Suite, then The Audubon Suite, and ultimately The Garden Suite. It quickly became a tasteful riot of lavenders and purples with roses everywhere. Down pillows, ruffles, bows, Audubon flower prints, sterling silver vanity pieces, an antique gilt-framed mirror and china bowl that had belonged to her mother combined to make this the most exquisitely feminine hideaway imaginable. We did see some preliminary wallpaper choices, but we were assured that the final choice was not among them. In fact, she would have beaten Catherine to the finish line, but her bathroom wallpaper – a crisp lavender pillow ticking stripe – was back-ordered for six weeks. Monica's quarters were evidently contained in the myriad boxes that were delivered on a frighteningly frequent basis. She left the door closed and stuck a paper sign on it saying, "Aloha Suite Under Construction." Accustomed as we were to minding each other's business, Monica's refusal to share her plans worried us a bit, but if it had somehow been awful, she would be the first to insist that it be done over. In retrospect, we had no reason to worry. Monica is a devotee of all things Hawaiian and has wonderful taste. It was very reassuring, however, to catch a glimpse of paint swatches in mango, lime, and glistening ocean blue. No question about it, this was the Aloha Suite, direct from the Tropics.

The centerpiece of Alex's suite is a stunning art deco chaise that just makes you want to pose naked. The suite is like a slice of Paris in the '20s replete with paintings, statues, and splashes of color against angular black and white pieces creating surprises everywhere. It nearly begged to be "Isadora's Suite." Just for grins, I tossed a copy of Dorothy Parker's Poems on the bed.

Rachel's suite stayed a disaster for a long time. She just couldn't settle on a single theme. Some of her brainstorms were deemed too metaphysical, some too controversial, and some just too plain weird. Ultimately, she settled on One World and, as expected, it continues to be a work in progress.

My suite is a dream workshop for all of my most loved projects. It has a desk that runs the length of the outside wall with cupboards above and below to house tools and components for my miniatures, dictionaries, my handy dandy cordless wondertool, the computer and some of my glass art materials. I keep one drawer empty to remind myself that something new and wonderful is just around the corner. I was concerned that no paying guest would choose such a utilitarian room, but when it adopted the name The Craftsman Suite, everything seemed to fall into place, and it definitely called for some junk shopping to round out the Craftsman style furniture I already had. Being on the corner, it has great light. Since then, several creative types have expressed enthusiasm about it. Whew!

If Catherine's kids are not the most generous, I'd like to meet the ones who do hold that title. Not only did they give us the piano we commandeered by wishing for it, but also evidently Catherine had chosen the previous weekend to talk with Lauren about the logistics of creating and maintaining a community sculpture garden. Lauren, being Lauren, included in the piano shipment a magnificent granite orb atop a scooped-out pillar. Her note referred to it as a seedling from which we could start a successful sculpture garden. When the delivery people had put the piano in place, Liz appeared as if on cue, bringing the piano to life. All joined in on Amazing Grace, which is almost sacramental to our little sisterhood. Much to our enormous pleasure, Liz can play the piano as well as she can sing. We all concurred that the piano could use a tuning and we put Liz in charge of finding the right tuner at the right price and almost immediately. Oddly enough, it appears to be easier to find a piano tuner in the country than in the city. You know that tradition has it that piano tuners are blind? Not so unreasonable when you consider the fact that they needn't see. Because we were forewarned, we even had on hand the traditional glass of port and a slice of seedy cake prepared in our very own kitchen especially for him. Never let it be said that we're not quick studies. The piano's arrival brought with it a renewed energy and spirit of confidence, where it might have been flagging.

Catherine's kids didn't stop there. They had purchased a ranch in Southern California in the hope that their children would take advantage of a non-urban environment in which they could cultivate social relationships and create legends all their own. They have horses, plenty of acreage, snow in the winter months, a swimming pool and, by now, a second house. I suspect that they live in gripping fear that the fun is going to run out before they've tried it all. Living in a world of opulence as they do, you might be prepared for a certain touch of greed, but there is not such a thing. And the best part of the ranch is that we have a standing invitation. So, like all things with which we furnish our world, the ranch has become ours. We all have the requisite boots and at least one plaid flannel shirt. Our Wranglers are suitably worn and the Ralph Lauren linens are perfect after a tough day at the ranch.

It is said that if you really want to know someone, travel with him or her. Travel we did. Local trips (less than four hours round trip driving time) interspersed with random trips to such places as Monterey, Lake Arrowhead, Northern Baja and Catalina Island whetted our appetite for travel, but nothing beats a trip across the pond...unless it's a trip well south of the border. The slightly more complex trips to places like San Miguel de Allende, Paris and the South of France kept our sense of adventure finely tuned.

The trip to San Miguel de Allende started creeping into our daily conversations in late March and by mid-April we had a crate of information about homes for rent, classes to take, restaurants to sample, chefs to employ, gardens and homes to visit, artists to spend time with and side trips to enjoy. Everyone agreed that May was the perfect travel month so we started there and narrowed it to early May for gardens, weather and fringe rates. You would have thought we were in a race for the last accommodations available. Anywhere. So we go back to the previously tested method of planning trips: ask the people who have been there for recommendations. There is one serious caveat: listen to advice only from people who share travel style with you. If, for example, you're talking to a late-twenties male who sports a black leather wardrobe and has lots of tattoos and the requisite body piercing and vocabulary to match, you might not be quite so interested in his favorite café that's only an hour and a half outside of town. But there is a possibility that his travels might be just exactly what you're looking for, in which case you might reassess your existing group.

Planning the trip to San Miguel was absorbing, but we had to remind ourselves that first and foremost we had this little seven thousand square foot project we'd committed to and we didn't even have a definite name for it, as Rachel had so gently reminded us regularly. But name or no name, our dream continued to evolve and crystallize.

Downstairs, we had a couple of walls added to separate the dining room and the library from the living room. The students, as planned, finished the surface preparation in the library and dining room first. We had decided to whitewash the satiny, newly sanded pine ceiling throughout The House, leaving the wood grain visible while capturing lots of light. The floors we decided to simply finish and maintain with tung oil, giving the assorted planks a rich patina without having to varnish every few minutes. The moment we put some diluted paint on a brush and then on the ceiling, we knew this was a good thing all the way around. It is said that our cheers could be heard across town. And our elation made us think that it might be time to hire a chef who could plan his or her dream kitchen from the gas jets up. We were quite certain that we couldn't last forever on fast food.

The talk around town and beyond was that we were six loony (probably lesbian) women who would doubtless overpay since we were "from the city." They had no clue that we were also tight as ticks. But that kind of rumor kept our List of Possible But Not Probable Employees quite long. They could not possibly understand that we were first and foremost concerned with impressing each other. This means that if one of us pays too much for something, she will be severely belittled and regularly reminded of her error. For a very long time.

Several local cooks and chefs stopped by every now and then to be sure they were still "on the list." Three of them seemed to be a cut above, so over the course of time, we got fairly well acquainted. For the most part, the selection was abysmal. One gentleman had a catering truck that he proposed to park alongside the house. He even offered to wash the truck's awning. Another, a woman, suggested that we should provide a separate brunch and serve frozen waffles with a variety of syrups. In her house, she claimed, such a taste adventure would be considered sensational. Yet another prospect specialized in German food but hadn't cooked any yet. And he really didn't understand the concept of a gourmet menu featuring only five or six entrees and changing daily. We really did want to hire locals, but they were not making it easy.

We had not yet thought to recruit Bert to pre-screen

applicants and to give us an objective rundown on the employability of some of these characters. What were we thinking?? Of course he knew everybody and pretty much all of everybody's business. And he had taken a liking to us. And it gave him great pleasure to protect us against such ne'er-do-wells and unscrupulous villains as those found in this bucolic valley. His first assignment was to review the list of wannabe chefs and make meaningful comments. Bert took his assignment very seriously. He put the list into a plain brown envelope he had brought with him. It was obvious that even a little tiny element of intrigue sweetens the pot immeasurably. "Whatever it takes" was the watch phrase of the day. We learned that the finalists were currently employed, residents of the valley, and well liked. Maurice was divorced amicably and his ex-wife and children had moved to the Bay Area, much to his dismay. Michael actually had a resumé that extolled his talents as a brilliant chef but made no mention of his private life. He was unavailable the day we did interviews, so he went into the Possible But Unlikely file. Vincenzo was firmly married to the love of his life, a beautiful Swiss woman who kept him reined in as appropriate. Both men had worked as chefs in the valley and surrounding communities. It was a toss-up: culinary skills or social graces…can't have both.

When we told the two finalists that they would participate in planning the kitchen, it was like a straight shot of adrenalin. From mincing prom dates to plantation owners in a flash. For the most part, they agreed on the kitchen basics and decided to work together on planning the layout of the kitchen. Neither knew which of them would get the nod, so they had to work in a state of constant compromise, an unnatural position for anyone with prima donna leanings. Their conversations were peppered with such high-end words as AGA, Viking, SubZero, Bosch and some that had never crossed my path. It was clear that our reputations were not based on frugality and if I had any intentions of finding "previously owned" equipment or appliances I could stop immediately. I had never seen Catherine scoff until I introduced avocado and harvest gold as color options for good, reliable, previously owned appliances. You would have thought I had deliberately wrinkled my holy cards. Seems to me that it's okay to do a miserable job using miserable looking equipment, but I was soundly out-voted. I promised myself that we would revisit this issue before we started buying faux antiques. Vincenzo and Maurice conspired to fatten us up for the kill. Every afternoon they each brought some delectable treat designed to sway our choice one way or the other. And we just stuffed ourselves. Thank heavens we didn't have the full kitchen in place. We did, however, decide that the chef did not need to live in. We sliced out a private nap room behind the kitchen for times he wanted to rest or stayed too late to drive home and get back for brunch.

The library took shape almost magically under the supervision of our resident reader, Monica. Journalist extraordinaire, she has written for major publications like the Washington Post, The Chicago Tribune, The New York Times, and The County and Coast Reporter. Oops. I didn't mean to cite that weekly journal, but it was one of her crowning achievements, after all. She is a voracious reader, having read virtually every book that has crossed her path. We agreed that Monica would be forever in charge of which books would find homes in our library. The first thing she did was to have a sideboard built to store games, including the classics: Scrabble, Monopoly, Clue, Yahtzee, Stratego, checkers, dominoes, cribbage, Trivial Pursuit and Chinese Checkers. And for the solo game players we stocked plenty of playing cards, jigsaw puzzles and books of crossword puzzles and Sudoku.

The library aside, Monica is, first and foremost, a mostly single parent of five children who simply adore her. They vacation together, promote each other's businesses, party together and solve problems together. Her peaceful approach to life allows her to observe, to consider, and to advise if appropriate. She is not, however, a prude. In fact, she could be characterized as sexy at any age. I'm not certain that anybody enjoys a roll in the hay like she does.

Rather than do something smart, like check Craig's List for local furniture and furnishings, we went straight to the Pottery Barn catalogue that said right on the cover: Design Your Dream Home. Okay, and thank you very much, we did. We took a field trip to shop Pottery Barn and Restoration Hardware from stem to stern, taking copious notes along the way. Not counting what we ordered, we ended our foray having spent an entire day and a total of $80 on two hogscraper candleholders and the pair of candles for them. More than that, we came away with an education and a vision of the library that pleased each of us. Our collective vision was of a peaceful, inviting room with rich, soothing colors and plenty of wood. The wood walls and shelves were stained a sexy new color called gunstock. The bookcases are built-in but backless, allowing the original wood and the doeskin paint on the new walls to remain visible. The higher shelves are served by a library ladder rescued from a gallery with imagination but not enough exhibitors. Not a bad excuse for a ten foot plus ceiling. We also invested in a plush, comfortable sofa and a russet-colored traditional leather chair. The game table could have been difficult, but a perfect specimen was calling our names from the great beyond we know as eBay. Liz and I had also seen one at a local shop that specializes in "reclaimed" wood furniture. As it turned out, the eBay table and the local table were one and the same, less shipping. For the most part, Robin's Reclaimed Treasures didn't feel much different from a junk store, but the beautiful hexagonal mahogany game table, with six comfortable, elegant balloon-back chairs that needed no refinishing, put Robin's in a class all its own. She obviously had no idea of the chairs' value and we didn't feel obliged to tell her. She was so pleased with our purchase that she called her husband at work to sweet talk him into delivering them in his pickup that afternoon. Among their other offerings they had several reclaimed/restored side tables and occasional chairs. I will admit that I have often wondered about those occasional tables and chairs. What are they the rest of the time? Do you suppose that occasionally they are footrests or ladders? That puzzlement aside, we promised that we would return for small tables and chairs.

We got back to The House early enough and excited enough to put a second (and hopefully final) coat of paint on the two new library walls and stain on the wood trim. The sofa and leather chair were not expected for at least a month, but serendipity was again on our side. Meredith, our Pottery Barn guru, called to say that the sofa we had chosen had just been put on sale as a floor sample with no marks or damage and would we like it delivered on Tuesday? Does a bear live in the woods? We went into a group frenzy with the sudden awareness that we would have one room virtually complete by Tuesday. FIVE days. Could we do it?? Daht ta dah. Nothing like a looming deadline to turn calm, capable adults into super heroes. We had settled into an easy but effective rhythm.

Liz, the anal retentive list maker, kept us on point. She posted her lists where everyone could see them and be driven to get in each other's way as much as possible. The to do lists posted that day looked something like this only they were long and vertical, making it look much more onerous than it already was. We donned our capes and became the best of the best. A six-woman team of rocket fueled over-achievers on a roll.

TO COMPLETE LIBRARY	
have hutch built	leather chair
have ceiling fan installed	2 side tables
paint, stain	coasters
throw pillows	waste basket
acquire books	tea cart
area rug	coffee table games
3 lamps	tantalus

Our celebration was cut a bit short with the welcome arrival, in Stan's pickup, of our beautiful, octagonal mahogany game table and six matching chairs. If there was ever a table with purpose, this was it. As we expected, Robin came with her husband, ostensibly to help but more likely to get her first-on-the-block report on our progress, our personalities and our sexual proclivities. Our neighbors just couldn't get their arms around the possibility that we were perfectly ordinary women, as women go. Much to our delight, Robin also presented us with a most thoughtful gift: two very attractive wood chairs from the shop that didn't even belong in the same hemisphere as the game table.

We made ourselves comfortable during the restoration with hand-me-downs, like the pair of beds Rachel was replacing for one of her bunko group, an apartment-sized refrigerator and microwave salvaged from a defunct business, and a good coffee maker. The House had wonderful, sweet well water, so anybody who wanted designer water was on her own.

We had asked our two chefs-in-waiting to draw up proposals for equipping the kitchen. We could increasingly hear raised voices and slamming of doors from the kitchen area, so we knew it was time to make our decision before Vincenzo and Maurice killed each other and we had to start all over. Maurice was a good sport about his second-place finish and started packing to move north, back to his ex and their kids. The winner, Vincenzo Bellini, was ecstatic. He presented their drawings and product information and projected costs (choke) for our consideration. He had also made preliminary contacts for installation, but we were perfectly happy with Scotty coordinating that sort of thing.

With the library complete except for the books and a few necessary purchases, we turned to the dining room, mostly because it seemed the easiest to tackle next: stain and finish two wood walls and the woodwork, paint the two new walls the same warm suede-textured brown as the library, buy drop leaf tables and a small sideboard for Vincenzo. Of course we needed to polish the magnificent 1920s brass kerosene lamp converted to a soon-to-be-glistening chandelier and the assorted wall sconces taken under cover of night from other rooms. We expected the most challenging element in this room would be finding a ten foot by fourteen foot rug, just large enough to protect the floor and minimize the ambient noise. The center dining table turned out to be very controversial. Round? Oval? Footed? Trestle? After days of debate, we voted on a round rosewood table with leaves that would allow it to seat fourteen. It was previously owned by a single lady, and it was a little dowdy, but clearly extraordinarily optimistic. Oddly enough, we found a perfect magic carpet online, but we continued to strike out on the four or five perfect drop leaf tables. Oh, well. Sooner or later they would appear. Of course it might be a little awkward to have our guests stand throughout the meal unless we bill it as a sacrament. But that might be even worse. So we dragged the trashed beach chairs out for ourselves, suitably ashamed, when Peggy pulled up in her pickup to offer us the use of ten dining chairs. Thank heavens!

7 These Kids Are Why People Keep Having Children

Possibly the most curious item in this house is the heavy iron o-ring hanging from the ceiling of what had been the master bedroom but now served as the dining room. At first glance, it is so out of place that it escapes the eye entirely. At second glance, its location over where the bed had been causes a bit of a brain flicker. We always check out the most conservative couples because they react predictably. Perhaps a swinging bed? A place to hang a light fixture? A place to hang a hammock? Think prohibition. Booze had to be well hidden but accessible in case the queen stopped by for tea. So the original owners dug out a space under the bedroom floor to store moonshine and store-bought. They covered it with an exceedingly heavy trap door and moved the bed over it. A rope and pulley were attached to the trap door, which opened to reveal libation as needed. And they entertained generously but discreetly. We turned right around and had a wine cellar large enough for 200 bottles of wine built in with access through the dining room. That should be enough to slake any thirst.

We were perched on the precipice of the single most terrifying adventure we might create for ourselves. Vincenzo was unfortunately in a demanding situation with no real end in sight. He felt completely manipulated and absolutely chomping at the bit. There he was, an actor with a starring role and no audience. Scary. I will say that he could have walked out in the middle of the Grand Opening dinner and he chose not to. He dedicated his energies to staying healthy in order to be able to find Maurice and clobber him.

The first major appliances to arrive were the two SubZero refrigerators. Despite the fact that they arrived ten days before we expected them, we were ready and more than willing to accommodate their delivery schedule. We had ice cream for dessert that night and plenty of ice for our drinks. Vincenzo had a master list and he did check with us on prices but mostly stayed his course. He located the best commercial kitchen supply store in the three county area. Naturally, we all wanted to go because it had the same sort of aroma of promise we felt in the Big Box even though the appliances were ordered. And going with Vincenzo was a great idea. That way it probably only cost five times more than it should have. So off we went, credit cards in hands. Thank heavens they have a delivery service! We bought full china, crystal, flatware and linen service for thirty, pots, pans, soufflé dishes, trays, cooking utensils, and bowls. In fact, our sleigh was so full that we sent up a flare for students willing to work during their spring break organizing the pantry and kitchen under Vincenzo's close supervision. It only lightly occurred to me that this was a tune-up for WilliamsSonoma-SurLeTable-LePetit-Gourmet – and any other kitchen store with "le" in its name. This is where we applaud our foresight in selecting glass fronted cabinetry so that we could go out and admire our acquisitions any time.

Vincenzo had some strong opinions (will wonders never cease?) about the public inauguration of the kitchen including an open house buffet, or a champagne reception, or a wine and cheese tasting. He almost won, but we prevailed, at least in terms of timing. First, we would have an outdoor barbecue on the patio honoring our student workforce and faculty and parents who were involved. We would take that opportunity to announce the accomplishments of the group, which ultimately numbered thirty-seven students, and to thank them in perpetuity by having them each carve his or her name on the porch. We had a little heartburn at the thought of having thirty-seven kids to The House to carve trip-and-falls in the surface of the porch, so I was duly pleased when it became clear that they had no intention of defacing their own work. They decided to carve their names within a foot of the house wall or a foot from the outer edge of the porch. They also proposed filling the carved-out names with dark wood filler. We agreed. No reason that part of the event couldn't be completed by then. After all, that would be nearly four weeks hence.

The fun of watching the parents, faculty and other adult hangers-on exploring The House in progress was a once-in-a-lifetime experience. The students were justifiably proud of their work, and there was a hushed undercurrent of gentle and not-so-gentle scolding or words of caution delivered from between clenched teeth as the students tried to keep their parents from being the first to leave a mark. In fact, they were so proud that they had created and developed a formal, supervised club at the school with a mission of maintaining the soon-to-be gardens around The House as a school project. They planned an herb garden as well as a flower garden and a small vegetable garden. They had even gone so far as to make arrangements for the 4-H Master Gardener to be their advisor. Work experience hadn't given them the nod…yet. And they had met with Vincenzo to find out what he would most like to have for his cooking. These kids are why people keep having children – in the fragile hope that theirs come out like these. All of the compliments went a long way toward healing the wounds of Vincenzo's long-standing and public snobbery towards people who work in agriculture and are not of Italian extraction. We think it's really that he doesn't like anybody who's not Italian. We explained to Vincenzo our relationship with the school and our indebtedness to everyone involved for their open-minded response to our original proposal, but the best reaction came from Vincenzo himself: "Why in the hell you didn't tell me? I can make a party they will remember when they are old. These kids are important and they need to know we think so. Now just stay out of my kitchen and I'll come tell you about the party tomorrow." I'm not sure that anyone had ever heard him string that many words together into a sentence, to say nothing about the subject being young adults and all of it being positive.

Deliver a party plan he did. You would have thought he was expecting to entertain the Pope. Explain as we might that we had a month to get it together, Vincenzo must have stayed up all night planning his debut Grilled Sweet Italian Sausages, Mushrooms Stuffed with Ricotta, Mozzarella and Pancetta, Ricotta and Spinach Fritters, Caprese Salad, Grilled Tuscan Steak, Bruschetta, Fire Roasted Red Peppers and for dessert, Panna Cotta topped with champagne grapes. We determined that he would audition each dish for us in the intervening month.

There we were in our lovely library having cocktails, but still with no mention of naming The House. As usual, Rachel had been pacing around outside, unable to be still. Suddenly, she burst through the side-door, crying, "Madrigal!" and gesturing frantically toward the horizon. "What on earth are you talking about?" said Monica. But Rachel just dragged us all out onto the porch and pointed at where the sky touches the roof. "See! Madrigal! Madrigal!" And The House was named.

8 The Foremen

In the back of my mind I kept hearing, "Staff…staff… staff…"

It is intriguing to note how much we can accomplish when we really don't want to do what we really have to do. We can clean a three-car garage thoroughly enough that we'd entertain there as long as the alternative is returning a phone call from a notorious whiner or a mother-in-law with a great idea for the kids' room. Of course our industrious efforts are rarely universally applauded because the easiest things to throw away usually have no discernible purpose and belong to someone else who lives in the same house. Batteries are a fine example. Some people can immediately and correctly identify a problem as a dead battery and then drop the offending battery into the box in the junk drawer "in case we need it." It's dead, dear one. That's why you took it out. "Well, leave it in the drawer in case we should need it in an emergency."

We had all managed staff in our other lives, so why was it so difficult here? Could it be that we just didn't want to be bosses right now? Or could it be that we were in an industry too tough for us? Not possible. Or could it be that hiring people would make us responsible when all we really want is to pretend. Not with real money or real customers. We'll be bosses, but very nice ones. Thoroughly benign. We would be excellent role models, provided our young fans didn't catch us pilfering additives like gin for our pre-dinner drinks.

So we did the sensible thing: we ran a little classified ad for hospitality positions, without too many pre-qualifications, and we were inundated with applications. We anticipated having two housekeepers, two kitchen and serving help, and one general labor type. With fifty-six applications, we had a clue about full time employment in the valley. There's too little of it to go around. First, we brought a dozen applicants to Madrigal, thinking that we should have an opportunity to see them in context. Ana, the first woman we interviewed, would never have seen the interior of Madrigal if I had been solely responsible for this hiring process. We had long ago ranked the applicants one to ten with one being the worst. The applications, sadly, were very heavily loaded with ones. The next one in the bunch was a nice looking young man, late twenties, who had some restaurant experience which, under further probing, turned out to be at a Dairy Queen in Visalia. The Visalia element was actually a plus because Visalia is lower on the food chain than Bakersfield. There's also a town named Weed Patch, a garden of scrub and cactus. That would ratchet Alex's Duchess title up another notch. However, he had aspirations to become a bell captain in a Ramada Inn somewhere and we certainly didn't want to interfere with his carefully laid plans.

We sent eleven of that first twelve home. We summoned another twelve and kept two in the short stack of maybes, including one who had to learn how to make a bed. We ultimately came up with five who seemed to fit, knowing full well that only time would tell. I certainly wouldn't want to work for six bosses. The group was to report for training the following morning at the crack of dawn. Monica would teach them all they needed to know. Maybe. Four of the five showed up. So our next step was a belated call to Bert, who could undoubtedly hear the panic in our voices. He came over as soon as he finished his rounds and started through the applications and our pitiful notes. We gave him an iced tea and left him alone. No more than thirty minutes later, he emerged, grinning ear to ear. Two of our selected five, it turned out, were moving to Vermont in a week. Another was our no-show. "You got real lucky on this project, ladies," Bert offered.

"The two that are moving east would have taken enough valuables to finance their trip, and the no-show couldn't make it because she's in jail today. The two that are left are fine folks, here for the long run. Even better, there are three you might have overlooked and they'll be great. I took the liberty of pulling out their paperwork. And I don't think you should try this alone again. You're far too generous in your judging, folks." We dispensed with all propriety and asked Bert if he would handle the personnel stuff for us.

Not that he knew any more about it than we did, but we'd rather have someone else to blame. The five he suggested and we agreed upon were gems, and highly trainable. The only hiccup in the revised staffing was discovering that we were all subject to severe, outdated gender expectations. Simply put, somewhere along the line we foolishly decided that beds should be made by female housekeepers and men were fit to climb trees and paint. Now that's a pathetic piece of nonsense. When we got it all sorted out sans preconceptions we had one female housekeeper, Socorro, and one male housekeeper, Percival, who had just enough peculiar about him that he went by "Val," insisting that Val was more macho-sounding than the customary "Percy." That may be true if your surname is Kilmer, but if you're slight and fair with wispy blond hair, you might want to shop around for another name. Or just make one up. The kitchen and serving help had never met before but by the end of the day they were fast friends, albeit from different parts of the world. Flora was from Central America and Socorro hailed from someplace in Mexico that wasn't yet all over the news with involvement in the drug wars. They both spoke Spanish and passable English. Their quick friendship may have been a result of not understanding a single word the other spoke or that their gestures were more than sufficient. The first time they got into a territorial catfight the answer was clear: gestures win. Their battles make a round of the dozens seem like child's play.

Not only did the decisions we took make the staff take notice, the decision-makers became instant heroes in town. Yet another side effect was that Becca and Tony became honored senior staff with no place to sleep. We firmly declined their suggestions that they put a motor home in the back forty. Having another "suite" a bit away from the house would certainly fit in with our long term plans, but we weren't going to go down easy.

For several days, Catherine had been a bit scarce and Frank had been his most mysterious self, humming and whistling like the old man walking down the next aisle at the hardware store. At cocktail hour, which we had re-instituted the evening we got the game table, Catherine produced, with great ceremony, the makings for Orange Blossom martinis and Waterford Lismore martini glasses. I vote for Catherine for chairperson in charge of party favors. She raised her glass to Frank in a lovely, heartfelt toast for his willing and able participation in this adventure and announced that Frank would be spending the night with her in the newly completed Orange Blossom Suite. She suggested that they be permitted to sleep late, but none of us would consider that privilege until we had a full tour of the suite. How she got so far ahead of the rest of us remains a mystery. It could only be those early days when she sidestepped working on the porch. The results were sensational, from the freeform headboard carved from orange wood to the linens custom-made from an early Marimekko pattern featuring green leaves, oranges, orange blossoms and California poppies. With large built-in closets on the dormer wall, they required very little additional storage, allowing for a beautiful antique lawyer's desk and two dressers in a similar style. In a fit of brilliance, our Catherine had purchased a huge roll of visqeen so that we could protect all of our goodies, especially the upholstered pieces. It seems the Dallas Deb was rearing her 'cleanliness is next to godliness' head. Lucky for us she's on our team.

Liz came to California from one of the Midwestern "M" states. Like most good midwestern Lutherans, she expected excellence from herself. She had to be not just cheerleader but head cheerleader. Not just CSF but top of the class. Not just an aide but honored as Most Valuable Community Volunteer for three consecutive years. However, she was apparently one of those women who, when she walks through a room in which there is a male, becomes pregnant. When she went for her "I'm a woman now" physical, her doctor admonished her as severely as he dared about chastity (if not, try caution). And then he told her she was pregnant. Thank you so much and how was your Tuesday? This situation is particularly frequent among cheerleaders whose entire job description involves making the athletes happy. The rest of us could choose a more virtuous lifestyle, or just be boring, looking down our cute noses, green with envy at the ones who got the nod for the squad. Always wanting to be the best, the most, and the first, Liz married the high school quarterback of her dreams. Unfortunately, the QB of her dreams had little in common with the one she married, who proved to be a thoroughly unworthy husband and/or father. So she took her baby boy and went west to carve out a life for themselves. She put her toe on the bottom rung of the corporate ladder at HoJo's and decided that hostessing was a lot like cheerleading. Come to think of it, so is managing money.

She wears the proper businesswoman banker clothes, drives the proper banker car and is escorted to the proper banker events by an appropriately proper banker man. And then you go on a proper banker winter vacation with her. First you try snow angels. Now that's easy enough. Then you try cross country skiing. You've seen the pictures and it looks pretty straightforward. But you spend most of your track time on your butt. That's not really true. You spend most of the time trying to stand up. You put your hands on the snow-covered ground, gracefully push your bottom up and your skis whip, leaving you again on your butt. You repeat this exercise, or variations thereof, several times, laughing audibly at yourself to prove to all that you are a good sport, while your thigh muscles are screaming for release. The only time your skis are still is when you cross the tips, which leaves you looking like a bolo knot. Meanwhile, the money manager charms a gentleman who claims to be eighty-three into giving us a free lesson. Which did me no good whatsoever because my muscles were in full revolt. Back at the house, we thought we'd take a shot at snowshoeing. Now that's a sport with some purpose: it makes everybody look incredibly awkward while getting from point A to point B to pick up a bottle of rum. Having seen her modest cross country skiing skills, snowmobiling sounded like a stroll in the snow. Not even close. I had completely overlooked the fact that in the "M" states they have real winter during which they use snowmobiles for all practical purposes like we use cars or, more accurately, like motorcycles. Which is to say as weapons. She puts her little, perfectly groomed self onto the snowmobile, puts her sci-fi helmet securely in place and morphs into a savage Beast of the Snow. Rounded down to the nearest whole number, she takes her machine smoothly up to about sixty-five miles per hour and whizzes by yours truly hollering "C'mon, you chickens!" Money manager, my foot. She's really a speed demon, bugs-in-the-teeth lunatic. It does give you pause when you realize that a schizophrenic type is taking care of your money.

Somewhere along the way, she climbed the bank ranks nearly to the top, scaring off her husband of many years. We all had theories about that: he had another woman, he'd found a man, he was really a hermit, he wanted her money…none of which helped his case, or hers. But when she started seeing him again after four years and a divorce, everybody had an opinion.

For some reason, the sisterhood found it entertaining to try to "fix" Liz. They spent perfectly good hours tearing her into pieces so that they could reassemble her with sexier lingerie, shorter skirts, nearly sheer blouses and spikier heels, all in an effort, presumably, to get herself a man. With that as a goal, the whole concept is suspect. I contend that if she wants something simple, like a man, don't worry about the underpinnings, go the direct route. Try "I'm auditioning for lovers. Are you interested?" Okay, maybe a little more oblique, but not much. Liz didn't have perfect luck with men, as you might have guessed. My personal favorite was the seventy-eight-year-old heel who met her for lunch and suggested that they take a cruise together even though she was "a little long in the tooth" for him. She left him sitting there.

As Madrigal got "finished," the need to have a plan for our grand opening grew large. All of us had at least a smattering of knowledge about marketing and we had no plan. Zero. Zilch. With the suites virtually complete, a name on the sign, the library stocked with appropriate reading and research books, and a chef and kitchen staff lusting after hungry guests, we had no excuse to put it off any longer. We staged a series of quasi meetings designed to drag a little more consensus into our futures. The first event, of course, was the barbecue for our students. That was a given. According to plan, we sent proper invitations to the thirty-seven full participants, selected parents and school administrators, and presented each of them with a polo shirt with the Madrigal logo silkscreened on the front. We also presented a sizeable check for the school. Then we served them unrivaled food, which they will forever seek and not find at lesser eating establishments. All in all, the barbecue was a huge hit. Especially when Rachel was presented with a Letterman's jacket proclaiming her MVP. We three only children in this group expect better treatment.

Remembering if you might that we only had Chef Vincenzo and five staff (plus Becca and Tony), and that their formal training started about thirty minutes before our first guest arrived, I must say that everyone played their parts superbly. We served soft drinks and a nice white wine and wafers with bar le duc while our guests settled in. With the possible exception of an adorable mouse that Socorro snatched up by the tail and launched half an acre away, the rural location was perfect.

The last guest gone, we settled into the library for a nightcap and a recap. What followed was fairly close to a disaster. Who would have imagined that planning for a fun event would transform us into bickering ugly people? We tried thinking through an afternoon event, and ran smack into football. Then we tried for a late afternoon event and locked horns with the religious element's Saturday bingo. It looked as though every specific date presented a conflict and every "general" date was likewise victim of some impediment. It took a writer friend of ours about two seconds to come up with a solution: a Saturday Champagne Brunch in the garden. This year it would be the Inaugural Mimosa Morning. Get them to Madrigal before they get into their bagged out Hawaiian shorts to trim the trees or fix something visible from the street.

No matter what the age of Hawaiian shorts or the person wearing them, they seem to hold a powerful fashion sway over their owners. They tether their owners in the front yard, enabling all of the neighbors to understand that somebody needs a hammer now... immediately...this very minute...and I mean NOW. They encourage the wearers to belch and fart at will. In fact, I can think of few things as silly-looking as a paunchy, balding, beer-drinking Hawaiian-shorts-wearing guy whose wife has just walked over to him with the new thirty-five-year-old neighbor in tow unless it's the fifty-six-year-old wife holding her eyelids up looking totally shocked – as if she'd been goosed in public. We believe with every fiber in our bodies that we can look just like we do in front of a mirror without the assistance of the actual mirror. Fortunately, Madrigal has no neighbors within earshot of the spoken word and the neighbors we do have are not candidates for tropical clothing.

Whatever the challenges were, the Mimosa Morning sounded terrific. We had to do some powerful persuading to get our students to allow anyone into the house for any reason whatsoever and the concept of having irresponsible adults loose in the house was just too much. Their pride of craftsmanship was warranted and admirable, but their sense of ownership was creeping up into the danger zone. After nearly an hour of pointless snipe shooting, during which we debated such critical issues as oldies music vs. country music, good champagne vs. potable champagne, and padded folding chairs vs. metal ones, we decided that a different approach to the planning process might yield better results. After all, we concluded, we put Madrigal together to please ourselves, not teenagers, no matter how terrific they are. If it pleases us, then it should please our prospective guests. For the time being, that's what it was all about. However, I'm still unsure about the redundancy of flower arrangements in a garden.

Bert, who remained a member of the family from day one, found his way to the patio and looked around at the changes with obvious approval. He would not have hesitated to make suggestions as long as they wouldn't hurt anybody's feelings. By the time I noticed he was shifting his weight from one side to the other, he looked decidedly uncomfortable, and not much older than eight. So I asked, "Are we missing something, Bert? What's up?" Bert responded with an "aw, shucks" kind of shuffle, blushing cheeks, and a smile we'd never seen, including a marvelous dimple on the right side. "Well," he said, "I never would have imagined in my wildest dreams that you could have done what you've done. You took this waste of earth and turned it into a real beauty." We tried to thank him for his kind words and his confidence, but he clearly had more to say. He took a couple of deep breaths and launched into his speech fast enough that he couldn't back out of it. "I've lived in this valley for near nine years now. I could've moved to the coast, but this is my home. I know the folks in this valley like family and I want to live here until my livin's done. There's only one little catch... or maybe a big catch. I been seeing a lady named Beverly McDougall, but she doesn't live in the valley. She lives about fifteen miles up the road. She's never married or had children because she didn't have time, what with taking care of her parents who just passed a couple years ago. (Deep breath.) You were kind enough to invite me to the Champagne Brunch and I was hoping that you would allow me to propose marriage to Beverly at the party in the newest and most beautiful place in the valley. I surely don't want to take away the attention Madrigal deserves, but if you could just give it some thought." Anything else he might have wanted to say was drowned out by our applause. He swore us all to secrecy and produced from his jacket pocket the engagement ring he would offer her. He handled it with the reverence due a first-on-the-block Decoder Ring. The collective gasp said it all. It wasn't in a proper box or on black velvet, so it wasn't displayed to its best advantage. But, really, how much does a three and a half carat diamond need? It turned out that Bert's mother saved her nickels and dimes to buy just such a moment for her son. After all, his sister had one almost as big and she had to go to the trouble of trading up through several husbands. Our answer to Bert was an unequivocal "yes!" We bandied about the process of getting her to come to Madrigal. That part was simple, and straightforward. Bert reports to Beverly that he has been asked to say a few words on behalf of the community at the Champagne Brunch and admits to her that he's nervous about spending social time with what amounts to his customers. She, of course, will assure him that she'll be right by his side and if he gives her the high sign, she will interrupt the conversation politely, rescuing him from any embarrassment. As Bert related the conversation the following day, she seemed almost giddy to be invited to the event. Little did she know...

While we were putting together information for our brochures and information sheets, an intriguing question came up: When was Madrigal born? Was it when the house was first built? No; for whatever reason, it started as a working cattle ranch and stayed that way. The rancher and the hands worked the land, ate in the house, slept in the house and misbehaved in the house. Basically, they treated the house like a bunkhouse. It was not unusual, for example, for ten or fifteen cowboys to spend the weekend when they'd had an afternoon of spontaneous rodeo. Not a formula for the Good Housekeeping Award.

As was common in the ranchos, the landowner might live on the property or not, but they did generally hire a foreman to oversee the operations. The foremen were tough and powerful and given to corporal solutions for most problems. The original owner of the property that included Madrigal was a man named Fletcher Hammond, who was apparently a little difficult to work for. He did hire a series of local housekeeper/cooks with colorful origins and names to match. Names like Drypockets, Shortbread or Bones. One did stay for almost two months, but was finally unhappy enough to leave abruptly without his parting wages. One would assume that someone had originally planned to have a family when the uncles sold out, leaving just one branch of the family to create the traditions and memories of the house. Or was it when we six ladies decided it was our dream? Close. I believe that a house is born when a woman first endows it with the virtue of hospitality, capable of providing peaceful rest and satisfying nourishment. I think this is true of suburban tract houses as well as houses with stories to tell. And it works for Madrigal.

The ranch was a rough and tumble place, very short on couth. It really needed some Russian shot putter with questionable hormone distribution à la Tamara Press to run the household. And so appeared Edna, the first "woman of the house" that became Madrigal. Homely, buxom but not shapely, schooled up to knowing her letters and numbers, strong as an ox but with a heart of gold, Edna was mother to eleven children, all under the age of ten, seven of them hers and the remaining four foundlings rescued from peril. She was filled with hope when she found the position through a domestic placement agency, which offered far too generous descriptions of the house and living situation. She and seven of her children arrived at the house late one Saturday in an unusually bitter, bone-chilling November aboard a perfectly horrid open-sided horse-drawn supply wagon, in which they had ridden packed around a couple of bags of grain and some ranch supplies. At least the bag of wheat was warm on her legs. She would never have guessed that she would be blamed for the loss of the wheat. They carried all of their possessions with

them, prepared to make a life on this hardscrabble piece of earth. By the time Edna was dry and had put her brood in their corner of the patio, her esteemed employers were fairly close to falling down drunk. It was, after all, a Saturday night, albeit a miserable one. And they could celebrate the additions to their troupe, which represented eight more people at whom they could holler orders. They were not exactly abusive (perhaps loud and demanding is better) and anyway, her expectations were appropriately low. Edna simply responded to the first few orders barked at her and then retired outside where she could not hear the mayhem as well. She didn't expect to ever be comfortable again. In fact, she made an effort to clean the children's travel clothing, or at least get the biggest chunks of mud off them. The project was a complete failure: very little dirt rinsed out and it took three days to dry anything in the overwhelming cold. Is there any reason she might have hated the place from the minute she got off the wagon? The wagon master practically shoved the little band off the buckboards as he left to complete his rounds. "At least," she thought, "we'll have a roof over our heads." Almost. Local lore has it that she and the children were allowed to sleep in the sheltered but exceedingly cold patio. Edna saw to their meals and kept them from being underfoot as much as possible. There are still elders in the valley who were around in the 1910s, and when Edna's name comes up, they just look down and give their heads a single shake. "She tried," they'd say. "Heaven knows, she tried." But then her options weren't so great either. Eleven kids speaks of careless behavior or determined desperation. Either way, they are a more than significant liability for an unmarried woman to carry.

The way these domestic placements worked, the employer paid the cost of getting the employee there, but if the employee wanted out he or she had to bear the entire cost. Close to impossible when they had little or no wages to save from. It makes it a bit easier to understand how mastery of the art of flirtation could be as important and effective as cold hard cash.

She lost two children to influenza in that first winter and was then allowed to move into the shed with the children to sleep. Mind you, that was after the second child's death, not the first. She grieved deeply, and sacrificed her iron will to survive. She gathered up her children and returned to the coast, probably using the same wiles that got her all those children. Through the years, people have reported seeing two young children on the widow's walk. We wonder if it's the same two "spirit children" occasionally heard whimpering in the shed.

When Edna left, the ranch felt oddly hollow, even though no relationships, positive or otherwise, had been forged during their brief stay. But the foreman had no doubt grown accustomed to having someone tend to the "women's work," so a search commenced. Flyers and public notices posted on windows were testament to Mr. Hammond's desire to have help. Hammond looked far and wide for exactly the right woman. She would have to be tough, gentle, strong enough to heft a bale of hay, not squeamish, have a cast iron digestive system, know how and when to ring a dinner bell, and how to prepare and tend a bath. He would also prefer that she not be particularly attractive, as "a certain allure slows the work worse than injury." Here we are, just over a century later, spending thousands of dollars each year to find that allure and use it to out-allure the next guy.

Enter Vivian. Admits to forty-two years old, looks sixty-five. Says she's a good cook, but we'll know that soon enough. Strong enough to heft a bale and the man holding it. Thin as a rail, so she wouldn't cost much to feed. Loves hot peppers, and "eats 'em like they was candy." Insisted on wearing her white apron, which seemed to give her supernatural powers, much like a precursor to Superman and his cape. None of us ever figured out how it stayed white and pressed without the benefits of laundry additives being available. Able to hold her own at horseshoes or roping. The perfect woman. So perfect that she ran off with one of the land grant boys. Next came Mr. Sanborn. Followed swiftly by Mother Adelaide, who was succeeded almost instantly by Sra. Domingo.

And then came Miss Crane, whose name and persona were as one. Miss Crane was extraordinarily tall, cursed with a skeletal body, a very long neck and a scratchy voice. She was young, not much over eighteen, and full of dreams and ideals and a commitment to better the world for the less fortunate. (That would be who?) Of course she would be a housekeeper/cook, but she really wanted to teach and she wanted to teach the horror subjects like mathematics and reading. The rumor spread like wildfire in all of the places in the valley that children gathered. The possibility of having a school in the valley could only be discussed in hushed tones for fear that talking about it would make it real. There were no potential students living at the ranch but they had plenty of space and the arrangement would give Mr. Hammond a certain honorable clout in local politics. It took Miss Crane almost a year of pleading, threatening, encouraging and promising, but she won the battle fair and square. Her Teacher's Pet was Joshua, who was born with a severely deformed leg, precluding his participation in most of the roughhousing and outdoor games. Fortunately, he was also born with a sunny disposition, a ready laugh, and a great mind, so other youngsters enjoyed his company and actually sought him out to play games like Chinese Checkers or even a sort of made-up chess. Otherwise, Joshua was the beneficiary of Miss Crane's free time. He flourished under her watchful eyes and was frequently paraded through the school planning meetings to demonstrate his academic progress. She managed to use some of Mr. Hammond's hard-working Basque ranch-hands to build a schoolhouse in time to open the school in January 1919. Then, when a student discovered Ichabod Crane in The Legend of Sleepy Hollow, Miss Crane's power over her charges multiplied tenfold. She was actually in a book! The children reviled her and were terrified of her. She was the star of countless scary stories repeated around campfires. But (and there's usually a "but") she did have control over the only place children could hide. There is plenty of evidence that attendance was much higher in Indian summer and the dead of winter. It occurred to us that Madrigal had followed a deeply entrenched tradition when we brought the high school into our family. With thoughts of our place in the history of Madrigal, we set our sights on our Grand Public Unveiling. There was little disagreement about generating our guest list: run a tasteful ad in the local papers, followed by a press release inviting the world at large.

There was, of course, shopping to be done, and where there is shopping, there is, inevitably, queuing. To reduce the boredom of waiting, you play a short game of

Tailgating, which is a lot like Achilles' Heel but confined to a smaller area: the checkout line. In a game of Achilles' Heel, you have the entire store to seek and find the enemy moving along up and down the aisles until something strikes your fancy and then you just stop without any warning. No pause or slowdown. Stop. Sometimes when you misjudge your distance and score a direct hit on the Achilles' heel of the nice man ahead of you, you look slightly abashed but insufficiently so. I believe that this is why we lean forward when pushing a market basket, so that when the person behind you runs into you, the basket hits your rear and saves your heel. These little wars go on all the time, wordlessly but with venom. I suspect that it is part of an unwinnable war born of territorial instincts about the sources of food. For several decades of their lives, women have control of the food preparation areas. These areas are corners of the world with little or no interest to men. Then, in sashays The Man on the back of retirement, who will go to great lengths to prove his culinary skills, investing small fortunes on built-in outdoor cooking and entertaining facilities, necessitating The Woman's relocation to some other quarters. Her authority of last resort seems to be the grocery store. We could easily substitute photos of grocery shopping women for pictures of the Roman gladiators hanging on for dear life.

9 Success or Failure

The week of our Champagne Brunch was a lulu. Everyone was tense, nobody liked anyone else's ideas, and there were definitely rumbles of dissent in the kitchen. Vincenzo had determined that he should have a kitchen staff of at least four, presumably so that he would not have to actually get his hands dirty. He was also having a bit of difficulty understanding the hierarchy of our little operation. In fact, he threatened to walk out the night before the event, but we bet that he didn't have the stones, and thank heavens we were almost right. We all agreed that threatening to walk out less than a week before the grand unveiling was tantamount to giving notice. There were no harsh words or raised voices; it just wasn't a fit. We really did try not to notice his behavior, but as we neared the big celebrations, we could no longer pretend that Vincenzo was part of our team. As we thought about it, wondering if we could have done anything differently, we concluded only that our use of the words "petulant" and "pout" set him off instantly and that there was no way to have made it work. We even went so far as to get in touch with Maurice, but he was having so much fun with his family that he had no intention of going back to work until starvation was just around the corner. More power to him.

Despite the ugly chaos backstage, the brunch went off without a hitch. The food was superlative, the students' autographs looked wonderful, Madrigal was definitely the place of our dreams. The prior three weeks spent dotting i's and crossing t's were worth every groan. Sixty people came to see Madrigal at her debut and we couldn't have been more proud. The day was picture perfect with a light breeze (so light it didn't interfere with the always delicate and quirky sound system liberated from a long ago radio station) and a crystal blue sky. The planting outside was obviously young but well planned to be beautiful but natural. The garden, produced exclusively by the students, was phenomenal. All of the plants were identified with appropriate signs, and herbs being used in the menu were identified with recipe information. The sculpture garden was a surprise to most and was very well received. The premier piece, the black stone globe balanced on a pink marble hand "on loan" from Catherine's kids, drew ooohs and aaahhs from guests of all ages, and the kids sent us a note accompanying an extravagant floral arrangement giving the sculpture to us as a gift. I overheard one of our students suggesting that they should have a sculpture component in the art classes. Hmmm.

The guests at our soirée included most of the city dignitaries, the business decision makers and the school community as well as the community known as "The Hills." The Hills was the first development in the valley and still holds considerable snob appeal, probably because the homeowners' association forbids overnight street parking of motorhomes and requires that every house have closed parking for every vehicle they own. Now if they could only ban wearing tank tops in public, we'd have something to shoot for. Whatever the reason, they came to the Mimosa Morning enthusiastically and full of compliments. We had placed a silver bowl in the library inviting comments and suggestions and had some excellent input. One idea we planned to implement right away was to build in a trophy cabinet to display awards won by our kids. The first trophy to be produced was The Madrigal Meets The Chamber Of Commerce Award, to be awarded by Madrigal whenever we like.

Bert was the logical emcee for the event, but he was entirely too shy for that assignment. Besides, he had other things on his mind. When we invited Bert up to the microphone, ostensibly to welcome Madrigal to the valley, he was alarmingly pale and a little shaky. He gave a lovely speech "on behalf of the community" commending our foresight and taste and the results. All of a sudden, Bert lost his voice. Gone. Lips moved but no sound passed between them. Catherine, in a flash of utter brilliance, saved the day. She quietly and quickly slipped into the library and returned to the table almost immediately, carrying four envelopes. She sashayed up to the mike and asked Bert to help her with the door prizes: a certificate for a massage, dinner for two, a gourmet picnic basket for two and one night's lodging. With all of the guests distracted by the door prizes, Catherine called Beverly to the head table and cajoled Bert, whose voice had miraculously returned, into taking back the microphone, whereupon he pretended to have dropped the mike and knelt on one knee, produced the ring in a proper black velvet and silver box, choked up a bit and said, clear as a bell, "Beverly, you know better than anyone that I am not given to being sudden, daring or frivolous, so you understand that I asked my friends and neighbors to join me as I do the bravest and best thing I have ever done. Would you do me the honor of being my wife?" as he presented the ring. Further explanation unnecessary. We thought she might faint, but she just cried and smiled yes! yes! yes! What a day it was. We offered them use of the garden for the wedding. Obviously.

We were simply unwilling to give up the beautiful day, so we didn't. We had lots of tricks left, beginning with croquet. We thought it best to play croquet early so that our guests would have plenty of time to forgive each other before heading home. Croquet is, you must know, a deal breaker. It's an "adult" combination of rugby and lacrosse, with polo sticks thrown in for good measure. How anyone could possibly enjoy a game for which participants must wear white pants and push a little ball through a wire hoop defies understanding. Lest you still think it sounds fun, or even interesting, we have several croquet rule books in the Madrigal Library to disabuse you of that notion. Everyone cheats and if money or a trophy is in the mix, the cheating is blatant. Our croquet court would eventually be green and manicured, but for now it was definitely rustic.

On the other hand, for the less aggressive, we had Madrigal Rules Bocce Ball, a therapeutic rendition of a time-honored sport. The pallino, or "p-ball," can be thrown anywhere it can be seen from the line, and the line is drawn by the next player up. The game commences when the p-ball is thrown. More laughter than skill is in order. Although bocce is usually played on a grass court, Madrigal Rules Bocce is intended to stay on the dirt. Clods and all. The rules are simple and intuitive.

OFFICIAL RULES & PROCEDURES FOR MADRIGAL RULES BOCCE BALL

1. Team members are determined by random draw. Husband/wife teams are not allowed unless their attorneys are present.
2. Team numbers are assigned in sequence as team members' names are drawn.
3. In the true spirit of Madrigal Rules Bocce Ball, matches will be played through the Championship Round according to the ladder, regardless of whether a team is undefeated or has lost a previous match. It is therefore possible for a team with a loss to play an undefeated team for the Grand Championship.
4. Each game will be played to 11 points. The winning team must win by at least 2 points (11-9 for example). A game with a score of 11-10 or 11-11 will be continued until both teams have rolled equally and one team leads by 2 points. That team is therefore declared the winner.
5. A "skunk" is a score of 6-0. When such a score is achieved the team wih 6 points is declared the winner and the team scoring zero is subject to mind-bending ridicule.
6. The playing area, including "out of bounds" areas, will be vaguely designated by the tournament judge and may or may not be made adequately clear to the participants. Any disputes regarding playing area and "out of bounds" shall be settled without excessive physical violence.
7. It is forbidden to steal, hide or kick your opponents' balls.
8. It is forbidden to intentionally drop a bocce ball on an opponent's foot.
9. Screaming as an opponent is about to roll a bocce ball is... well...up to you.
10. Physical abuse of the tournament judge (or his designee) is forbidden, as is verbal abuse.
11. The tournament judge's opinion (or his designee's) decisions will be final. Bribes are both acceptable and encouraged, but must be made discreetly.
12. Alcohol impairment is not an acceptable excuse for unsportsmanlike conduct such as distracting other players by making rude body noises.
13. No mooning or flashing.

AND A GOOD TIME WAS HAD BY ALL.

Just about the time the breeze freshened, the hilarity seemed to move back to the patio and indeed it deserved to. The youth contingent had become a sea of gyrating figures unrelated to one another in any way. Bless the headsets and earphones. Our guests were truly comfortable here. I think that anywhere people dance with their eyes closed can be deemed comfortable. On the flip side, places where they really need to keep their eyes open, whether to protect territory or to style-check the crowd, will never be truly comfortable places. These kids were actually dancing to their perfectly awful music in complete silence. This, I believe, is an excellent application of contemporary technology. Shortly thereafter, Billy Jack, local plumber, quietly asked Monica if he might play the piano. And of course she encouraged it. We ladies, new to the neighborhood, had no idea what to expect, so when those rough, gnarled fingers lit like butterflies on the keys we were speechless. He was transformed. We were transfixed. No longer could you see that he was wearing his clean but well-worn coveralls or his work boots or his ball cap. You could see him elegantly dressed in a tux playing the piano in a concert hall. After a couple of breath-taking classical pieces, he beckoned our Liz to join him, which she did, graciously and well. Their music segued into the popular music of the 40s and 50s, encouraging everyone to join in, except for our dancing teens, who looked even more disconnected with the rest of the world singing You Are My Sunshine and Two Little Owlies and Streets of Laredo. And, pray tell, who is able to leave a party when Brick House is being played or Creedence Clearwater Revival is filling the air? That was quite a moment when some bleep in our collective cosmic psyche recognized that a shift had occurred, all of a sudden, like watching for the time on your watch to change in Jackpot, knowing full well that it won't budge until you look away. Just that fast, grownups, but we were the grownups. Our tastes would prevail for whatever length of time we could hang on to the title (assuming we wanted to). The first question we needed to answer was "Can we be trusted as the grownups?" We concluded that trustworthiness was probably not our long suit, but we had experienced enough misbehavior in our late teens and early twenties to enable us to fake it. It got to be that time: the last of the guests were moving toward the door and the guests still within earshot tossed congratulations back over their shoulders. We told Billy Jack that he was welcome any time, whether or not we had guests in residence. He was flattered and promised to wear "nicer clothes" for when he played. Although it might have occurred to us, it wasn't something you could just demand, especially of a volunteer. We insisted that we pay for his "music clothes." And he agreed. Yet another little nod of approval from the patron saint of people who inadvertently succeed while they're trying not to fail.

As much as we would have liked to throw our shoes off and flop in the library or in front of the fireplace, we had work to do. Our first B&B guests were to arrive shortly after lunch to stay in three of our suites and take an exquisite picnic lunch with them the following morning. Omigod. Here we are. Let the games begin.

10 Off To A Tenuous Start

It's not as though we actually registered our first guests as guinea pigs, but it certainly would have been appropriate. Not only did we have to hang on, we had to look like we planned to be there and enjoyed it. Liz observed that it seemed a pity that we were having such a great time just minutes prior and now we were thrashing around in panic. Not a wink of sleep to be seen on the horizon for a few days. With our staff fully trained with about sixteen hours under their belts, we launched into our future. We may have disembarked one stop early or one stop late, but it was clear that we were off to a tenuous but committed start. Socorro was the most anxious to learn everything about the business with fantasies of becoming Ivana Trump. Unfortunately her tutors – us – knew much less than she did, so her best source of information continued to be People Magazine, which we should all admit is the only reason to go to a doctor's office. Otherwise, you might spend your entire life not knowing who's sleeping with whom and why they got divorced if everything was so hunky dory just a few weeks ago. And where they get those names for their otherwise healthy babies. Most important, how to keep your partner's sexual energy on high twenty-four seven.

Nobody has contacted me or anyone I know to find out if we are equally enthusiastic about having a perpetually locked and loaded heat-seeking plaything poking around without a break here and there.

Our guest rooms were perfect. No amount of fiddling with them could have made them more so. (Which is not to say we could resist fiddling just a little bit.) Catherine and Frank had mostly been "in residence" in the Orange Blossom Suite for two weeks, so we had our own soft opening and found our preparations to have been everything we hoped for, down to and including Catherine's lavender and orange blossom sachets. Liz had put a beautiful scented silk rose across a pillow on the bed in her voluptuous Garden Suite. My room sported a three-dimensional wood puzzle for a guest's amusement, but the power tools were stashed in a locked cupboard. Judging from comments by people who just stopped by for an early tour, the Craftsman Suite needed to be warmer, so I picked up a few period pieces and two Native American throw rugs. Isadora's Suite was to crystal and shiny things what The Garden Suite was to flowers. The suite invited its guests to share martinis in glasses from The Algonquin amidst dozens of sparkling candles. Alex had also set up an extravagant champagne tasting on the marble- and mirror-topped dressing table. It was absolutely Alex's style. Rachel's suite had a hushed feeling: lots of soft greens, bamboo (including the linens), and a graceful tea service on an antique teacart. Guests were encouraged to sample the teas and imported cookies. Monica's Aloha Suite, which she chose not to unveil until the day before we opened, fairly exploded with tropical patterns and colors. So artfully had she combined live flowering plants with silks that the lines between them were obscured and the fragrance in the room was surprisingly subtle to be so lush. Two sarongs were draped on one of the chairs. Perfect. And we were ready to roll as long as nobody let the cat out of the bag with our little problem of having no chef. When our first guests, Barbara and Jim, arrived in Hawaiian shirts, there was no question about their suite; to Tropical Paradise they went blissfully without even looking at the other suites. The next couple to arrive was Marti and Dave, an aunt and uncle of one of our students and winners of the night's stay awarded during the Mimosa Morning. Marti and Dave invited their best friends, CJ and Laurie. They were local but, more important, they were also members of a group of sixteen intrepid couples who spent one weekend every other month sampling B&Bs, making copious notes and sending the critiques on to a member-based nationwide travel club. Laurie confided that ours offered the best facility, menu and programs they'd seen. Now they were just hoping the food measured up. Oh for heaven's sake, why wouldn't it? We've only been cooking for family and friends for something more than thirty-five years. Actually, there was no reason we shouldn't knock their socks off! CJ and Laurie chose the Garden Suite after much hemming and hawing, threatening to never leave it once they had unpacked. Marti and Dave scouted the rooms and grounds and chose the Orange Blossom Suite for this weekend, promising to return until they had stayed in all of them – exactly the guests we were looking for! CJ was busily studying the bocce ball court and calling to Dave to join him. Oh, yay.

We did become peripherally aware of our serious problem several seconds before we opened: we shall call it prior planning. We had twelve beds in the six guest rooms, two in staff quarters, one huge sofa and several non-sleeping chairs. That makes fifteen sleeping places – max. We could have twelve guests or twelve owners in the total seven beds. Something was amiss – like a potential shortfall of fifteen beds. Do we hope to have only moderate success, keeping the rooms as available as possible? We call for a Madrigal library meeting after dinner. It's not a traditional time for goal setting but then we've never been accused of traditionalism. And it needed to be resolved. No matter how we moved the numbers around, we came up short on beds/guests. So we have to have some dreaded rules. To begin with, all guests and owners must make reservations. We can reserve all six suites if we like, but we have to make a reservation. On the other hand, if we have vacancies less than two weeks out, book 'em, owners or not. Suspecting that owners would mostly prefer weekdays when conflicts would be less likely, we declared this meeting to be concluded – or at least dragged on until later.

11 All Business In The Kitchen

It isn't as if we hadn't tried. Both Vincenzo and Maurice had worked supervising food preparation in the kitchen for a week, serving to us, our closest friends and family members not so much to test their cooking skills as to test their ability to work as part of a team. Maurice was clearly a better team player, but Vincenzo's drama couldn't be denied. Or so we thought.

From the very beginning, when Maurice and Vincenzo were just bringing us samples for tasting, Catherine, Rachel and Monica had sworn that Vincenzo was trying to kill us by serving delicious, calorie-laden food loaded with trans-fats. Alex and I thought he was wonderful. Liz sort of perched on the fence on this issue. Of course, Catherine, Rachel and Monica won. This group of crazy women would stand in as Chef Hydra until we found the perfect chef for the job. Out with Vincenzo and let the search begin for a chef who had mastered vegan cooking, wild game preparation, seasonal cooking for the hormone impaired, cooking around various allergies (imagined or real), and 101 uses for yam cream. Everybody wanted in on the decision, so we agreed on a Monday for the interviews and ran a classified ad in four or five local papers and Craig's List. We had complete confidence that our prospective chefs would transmit their resumés in advance and would appear as if by magic at the appointed time on the appointed day. And be willing to work hard at substandard pay. So when Rachel said she had a possible replacement for Chef Vincenzo from the previous round, we were more than curious. Oh my.

His resumé said his name was Michael Saracino. I've always liked the name Michael. Not Mike, which conjures visions of a slightly pudgy pre-pubescent boy or his thirty-five-year-old counterpart with the keg in the refrigerator. Certainly not Mikey, at least in part because of the commercial that said "Mikey'll eat anything." Not Mickey, for obvious reasons. Michael. It sounds finished and firm, but still warm. From the preliminary excitement of finding the resumé with all of the necessary contact numbers we plummeted into a depression that could only be brought on by one telephone message: "That number is no longer in service." Period. Not some little feel-good line like he'll be back within the month. And why would it be? Off Liz went to try to locate Michael's then-landlord and, sure enough, the For Rent sign was still posted, with the phone number. From there, the path led to the property manager and then to a lady friend of Michael's and ultimately to Michael himself. He had an aura about him that made me certain he could keep a secret. If I were in the hunt, that's a quality I would definitely look for.

Michael Saracino. Michael-with-the-incredible-blue-eyes. Michael-where-was-he-when-Liz-was-on-the-hunt. The interview was longer than it needed to be, for obvious reasons, but this man had a story and I couldn't get it out of him. At least not with all of us there. Otherwise, how would he have gone from being the fastest luncheonette chef on Tenth Street in New York to this bucolic little valley tucked away in the mountains of California? And why would he be looking for a job at an unknown inn rather than some fancy, fast-paced trendy restaurant in the city? I like to think he was on the lam, but his version was much tamer and appealed to the gentler souls among us. His brother, also in the restaurant business, had made his way west but had some financial difficulties. As expected, brother Michael came west to lend him a hand and stayed.

First, Rachel called him Mike, to which he evidently bristled, and he said gently, "I really prefer Michael if you don't mind." I looked to see if she was willing to give me the victory in a long past argument about nicknames, but she breezed on by. She came back with the heaviest volume of the Gourmet Magazine Cookbook and half a dozen copies of bio-friendly mood-altering season-sensitive health food magazines. Beyond our collective dreams, he was familiar with everything she challenged him with and then some. Of course, the fact of the matter is that suddenly none of us cared one whit if he could cook. It would be nice to just look at him and to hear him chortle when something known or unknown amuses him. And then there's his velvet laugh, which occurs without warning. The way Liz described its effect on her: "It's just like when you're traveling on some fifty miles of deadly straight smooth road, and you come upon a dip that makes your stomach feel weightless." This could be serious.

He turned out to be all business in the kitchen, though he could have posed a sizeable threat to our harmony if he'd been less ethical. We'll probably never know if he really had a serious lady friend "up north," but you can be sure that she protected him. Brilliant meals, thoughtful nutrition and happy sounds from the newly created kitchen. The disappointment was palpable. But I was fairly certain that Liz's long dormant libido was stirring, and indeed it was not many weeks before she arose from the dinner table one evening and, with a stern glance at the rest of us, declared, "Don't follow me," and moved smoothly into the kitchen.

Nothing was said, then or at any subsequent time, but Liz could occasionally be seen with a particular glint in her eye and a reminiscent smile.

With everything running so smoothly, (read: there's hardly any traffic tonight, can you believe it?) you can imagine our surprise when Becca, who was never seen before 10:00 am, came into the kitchen during the morning confab with that bright, slightly playful, off-to-places-unknown half smile on her face. We knew instantly that she was pregnant. That would account for it. But how could we possibly have missed it? The easy answer was the incorrect answer. We were wrong. Instead, she and Tony were leaving us almost immediately for Hayfork, Louisiana to help her Uncle Zeb care for one of the seven living sisters in that generation. She and Uncle Zeb weren't sure which one was dying of cancer, but there was no doubt he could use the help whoever it was. He was pretty much a pig, but a pleasant one and rarely defensive. One of the family jokes was that Zeb thought that the line into the laundromat was served alphabetically and his name never came up.

We tried to caution Becca about hitchhiking and talking to strangers, but she tactfully reminded us that she had spent lots more road time than we had. She would be dearly missed for her sense of drama and her tuna casseroles, created whenever Michael had to be gone at dinnertime. Sometimes the casseroles even contained tuna. Maybe too often.

12 Expectations and Murphy's Law

The morning off-the-cuff staff meetings in the kitchen were an excellent use of unstructured time. They were not scheduled. There was ample time for gossip, thinking up new twists for old recipes, maybe sharing a little news from the "outside," and adjusting duties and times. Michael made a little reversible sign for the kitchen door which said on one side: OWNERS WELCOME and on the other side OWNERS ENTER AT YOUR OWN RISK. It may not have made a real difference, but anyone passing through that doorway certainly had fair warning about any impending battles. Becca and Tony insisted that they didn't want a fancy farewell dinner, but were genuinely flattered that Michael had, in fact, offered. We all crawled out of our beds in the morning expecting to see a note on the Library table in Tony's exquisite hand and there it was. Obviously done together merging their memories, expectations and dreams. And planned for some time given the length of the note. I will always remember that they felt unable to take their leave in person because Madrigal meant love to them. And they hoped to come back someday to "show us that they deserved us." They promised to send photos and e-mail when they could, but all we had heard about Uncle Zeb indicated that he was not at the cutting edge of technology. I'm not going to start holding my breath until that's a little more likely.

We each had cleverly and very surreptitiously slipped some cash into their pockets and duffle bags, ensuring that they wouldn't starve or sleep in a cardboard box that first night. We were also fairly certain that they wouldn't discover our largesse until they got hungry. Sure enough, a young man headed in the opposite direction came to the door the following afternoon with a paper napkin from a diner on the interstate on which Tony had written: "Five-star diner. Thank you for putting us in touch with life as it can be." Good kids.

That first weekend at Madrigal should probably be written up and put in the hands of all those village idiots who think hospitality would be a fun way to make a living. Hospitality is a guaranteed invitation to showcase Murphy's Law, which goes something like "If it can go wrong, it will." Our guests were very generous with their praise but there were too many understood excuses to be made. For starters, nobody could find our fancy, schmantzy coffee, so we served crappy generic grind-your-own-beans-yourself coffee too late to do any good. We did promote a little of my home-made kahlua. The breakfast buffet was acceptable, but lacked the garnishes and food art that would take it up a notch. Michael was frustrated, mostly because he wasn't pleased with his own corner of the world. But his solution was perfect: mimosas all around the porch. The heat in the Library malfunctioned, leaving us whining for air conditioning, which we didn't have. One of the bathrooms developed a leak ultimately requiring professional attention. But, whatever the difficulties, everybody survived it. And the couple from Pasadena made a reservation for four rooms for three nights the following month. Can't beat that.

Then, when the conversation allowed for it, Socorro, Val and Ana brought in the three picnic baskets, as lush and appetizing as anyone could imagine: fresh French bread baguettes, designer meats and cheeses, fresh fruits, lovely flatware, properly large linens and glasses. Val was carrying the case of wine from which they were to choose their mid-day libations when he lost his grip on the box, dropping all twelve bottles on the hardwood floor. Our guests turned into a tableau of horror while the staff launched quietly into a blame fest. Some people, mostly men I hazard to say, are simply unable to get to a next step until they have assigned blame to someone... maybe anyone. Perhaps it's carefully carried in one's DNA, practiced frequently, and shined up regularly like badges. The infraction can be miniscule or huge but, until someone has either accepted the blame or agreed to share the blame, no forward progress can be made. That's why the expression "My bad" was so readily accepted. It is short and easy to toss into a fray when all you really need is permission.

Our inaugural guests made themselves at home so quickly that we appointed ourselves second in command. In fact, we decided after a rapid-fire abbreviated discussion that we would include them in the kitchen insofar as they wanted to join in. It went something like, "Alex, whaddya think?" "Why not? Even if they just did dishes." "The guys?" "Hell, yes." "Just make 'em sit down while everybody eats at the same time and at the same table and they'll think it's a vacation activity." "You guys are nuts," proclaimed Liz. "Do we sneak up on 'em? Or ask if they want to join in the fun?" "Actually, I have both corn to shuck and fresh peas to prepare," Monica offers. "I say we start our kitchen duties and see who wants to help. This could be good! And who wouldn't want to work in this kitchen?"

Actually, I had spoken to Michael about the possibility of relinquishing his kitchen guru position because it was so fraught with peril this first evening and he, unlike any prima donna ever born, thought it was a keen idea. On one side of the menu, there is a brief history of Madrigal which closes with the observation that almost all our menu items include ingredients that are fresh from our own garden. Honest.

The dinner menu choices were spectacular...

MADRIGAL
Inaugural Celebration Dinner

STARTERS

Select one

House Caesar salad
Freshly baked honey bran muffins
Onion blossom
Mini veal ravioli

VEGETABLES

Select two

Turkish zucchini
Butternut squash cakes
Creamed spinach
Fresh heirloom tomatoes, baked
Polenta with sun-dried tomatoes and capers
New England corn pudding

ENTRÉES

Select one

Boeuf bourguignon
Wild caught salmon with sage cream
Pasta primavera
12 oz. corn-fed bone-in ribeye steak

DESSERT *(A surprise)*

Save room for a memorable creation by Chef Michael
or choose from our special dessert cart

But the biggest surprise was our kitchen "staff." Everybody wanted in on the Open Kitchen, which was rather like a pot luck with no budget in a brand new dream kitchen subject to a predetermined menu. Harmony ruled.

13 Stardom Doesn't Help With Manners

Humans are like no other creatures in providing amusement for ourselves, except possibly the huge number of monkeys who also strive to be interesting. Don't we all know someone who is a dead ringer for a howler monkey? Especially in the morning? Or some bothersome youngster just like those thieving little Capuchin monkeys? Or the huge gorillas in captivity with nothing better to do than pick their noses and study the rewards carefully? It is said, even accepted, that people either obtain dogs that look like them, or they grow to look like them. When it's a bulldog owned by the stocky sheriff of a nearby county, it is humanly impossible not to laugh. When it's a basset hound owned by a droopy eighty year old or a "snack dog" just big enough to think it's a dog, you can probably just look away. But when FiFi came to call, there was no doubt where she'd been or where she was going. No question. Both she and Phoebe (her owner) are elegantly composed. With their commanding stride and ramrod straight posture it was pointless to wonder if FiFi was looking down her nose at you. She was. And when the pair walked past Madrigal after their afternoon events, the dog (for lack of a better word for cargo) FiFi steps outside the little picket fence so as not to soil her pedicure. FiFi and her mistress/keeper have their hair done just before her pedicure every Friday, which is really gross because her pink skin shows through with a slightly embryonic cast. One time – and only one – I sneaked up on a group of the Junior High kids and affixed a lime green puffball to a poodle's backside. Since then, every time I see a display of those puffballs I am reminded how satisfying it is to make an eighth grader laugh. Not much can compare. Then, just when you think you've figured it out, you learn that there is no such breed as a Royal Standard. It's really just an overgrown Standard poodle. The powers that be are working on it and if they are successful the world will be blessed with five sizes: Royal, Standard, Medium, Miniature, and (picture this) Teacup. But in the meantime, FiFi takes the cake for poodle level snootiness.

The only clue we had that FiFi might have a sense of humor right up there with the best of them happened when Fifi and Phoebe were on their way home on a lovely Saturday afternoon while four of our students were excavating a hole that might one day be a koi pond but at that moment was simply an adobe mud hole. I looked at the kids, hoping their clothes were disposable. The kids looked at me, the dog looked at the kids and – I swear this is true – backed up half a dozen steps and launched itself directly into the middle of the pond and rolled. I thought Phoebe might faint, but instead she did the oddest thing: she took off her shoes and waded just up to her ankles in the mud. Dog owners beware: this is a nuthouse.

When the Daimler pulled up right in front of the house and a piglet–faced uniformed driver stepped around to let the lady and her companion out of the car, every window in Madrigal was occupied – discreetly, of course. There are some things you just know, some things you're pretty sure about, and some you maybe don't want to know. From the lady's body language and the tone of her voice, you knew she was very unhappy about something specific but chose not to talk even though she really wanted to rant and rave. I am certain that all she needed was a good case of gluten allergy to make her the perfect guest. Her companion, Charles, who turned out to be a blowhard of the first magnitude, was happy to oblige. She had such control over her plans that a little misstep was a catastrophic event. She was used to getting her way. So much so that when she arched her eyebrows, her entire body arched. It reminded me of shower curtain hooks. In the absence of peers with whom they could force themselves to converse, they retired to the library, rudely closing the door behind them while they waited for a non-existent room to become available and continued their battle royale. Alex and Monica determined that the Daimler Duo would be troublesome guests at best. Back at the library, we explained to them one more time that we were full before they arrived and we had been trying to help, even contacting other lodging facilities, to no avail. When Charles raised his voice too, we were sure that body parts were soon to follow. Had he been just a tiny bit more offensive, we would have called upon some of our less ladylike vocabulary and behaviors, but he saved us the trouble, abruptly turning on his heel, firing a raw invective our way and stomping up the path like a goose-stepping German soldier. We weren't the least bit sorry to see them go. They were fast enough on their feet that we missed charging them for the several drinks they consumed, but we decided that they deserved each other. It was easily an hour before Socorro recognized the departed guest as the show-stopping Dierdre, currently everybody's up and coming bad girl music star. In this very house. In this very room. If the tabloids were correct, she was to have sat at a front table at the big music awards event on the night she stopped at Madrigal. No small wonder she was unhappy. Oops. Too bad she didn't ask. We could have helped.

There are many talents required in the hospitality field, all designed to reflect gentility and refinement. One is getting rid of rodents and roaches without being seen. Another is towel and napkin folding, which represents the highest or lowest form of origami, depending on your perspective. Whoever created the gentle art of napkin and towel folding no doubt earned shame for himself and his family and their descendents evermore, surely confining them for eternity to the hottest part of Hell. Being responsible for folding linens in dozens of shapes created a little gem of talent that could keep staff busy for ages. My favorites, at least in part because their folds made it easy to smuggle cigarettes, were the Water Lily Fold, the Iris Fold, the Petal and Fan Fold, which always sound like they could be used for after dinner entertainment as well. But trust me – there are dozens more. And of course you must be certain that you are using the proper napkin or towel. There are folds that go into glasses, folds that use napkin rings, folds that work on hand towels and folds that work best using two contrasting napkins. You get the idea. It's only fun the first thousand folds. And it isn't really difficult to do. And it does dress a table. But you have to wonder, "Why?" Dorothy, the head of housekeeping, had a rather strong opinion about decorative folded napkins: "Put the folded napkins on the table, ladies, lest the guests think you're in dangerous financial straits." Or, "Napkins can add a lovely splash of color when you can't afford candles."

Those of us who saw a certain amount of absurdity in folding linens had an ongoing and unspoken folding competition which even Dorothy couldn't resist. Every now and then, a particularly lovely napkin or towel would appear and someone would place a card on it reading "9.5." Likewise, a crumpled towel might earn 3.5 points. Amazing the shapes and illusions you can create with a simple square of fabric. I'm thinking, for example, of the Danish Candle Fold. But where did it ever get so morbidly boring that the last three squares on a nearly empty toilet paper roll cried out for decoration?

14 Opening Night

Rachel's suite, named One World, is very Rachel. As she learns new things about energy, wellness and our connections to the spiritual world, she applies them to her life, and the lives of her friends, making it very fluid but somehow consistent. She actually has two suites. One, upstairs, follows the patterns set for the other five suites. Downstairs, in the west wing, we created Harmony Suite, a quiet, soothing environment for massage, which will serve as a treatment room until such time as we need to enlist the aid of a live-in medical caregiver. It comes under Rachel's purview and, of course, appointments depended on her availability. Her suite is slightly smaller than the upstairs suites, but compared to the usual Spartan folding massage table/metal chair motif which looks suggestively temporary, this is a room fit for royalty, especially royalty who had been massaged on one of those portable tables designed in such a way that you always feel like you're in a marching band with your nose just a shade too close to the person ahead of you. The built–in cabinetry in Harmony Suite comes close to matching the library. One whole wall is a sideboard with glass fronts, locking cabinets, marble counter tops and a set of antique apothecary jars. Her reading material says nothing about magic, just the latest in wellness and natural healing. It was so perfect that none of us could resist sharing in the purchase of some bling for the lady: a pristine set of brass apothecary scales Monica found online. We rationalized it as connected to her upcoming birthday, just seven months down the road. So how on earth could we resist buying her a very early birthday present? I'm particularly fond of the massage table, which is topped with a Tempur-Pedic™ mattress and can be moved in all directions on a pivoting joint. It weighs a ton, but once installed it's as state-of-the-art as it gets. The masseuse can move it around, tilt it, turn it or secure it with a finger tip. Upstairs, the One World Suite is just slightly smaller than the others and features soft, soothing colors like sage, pale mango and wheat.

There is peace in the valley, but there is also plenty of room for surprises. On one relaxed Tuesday morning, Janet, who cares for a number of horses in the valley, paid us a visit. The first clue we had that something unusual was in the wind was that she knocked on the kitchen door rather than coming right in. It seems that our "next door" neighbor, whose house is a brisk mile-plus walk from Madrigal, is at a real intersection where complete strangers, seeing well-cared-for horses, occasionally abandon their own no-longer-wanted horses, leaving them in the hands of fate. It didn't happen often, but when it did happen, the task of finding yet another horsehouse fell squarely on Janet. That's a miserable stunt to pull on anyone, especially the horses. Janet looked hopefully at us and was met with a unanimous refusal. End of subject.

Except for Rachel, who forgot that she was not allowed to adopt any four legged pets, with the possible exception of getting a good mouser or two, which of course Rachel couldn't get involved in because she feels so sorry for the mice. One evening without guests, I strolled through the Library with a dead mouse on a paper towel and asked nicely where anybody thought we ought to dispose of the body and was nearly chased outside. My rejoinder to their threats was something like, "Fine. And I'll let every snake in while I'm out there." That seemed to restore our focus.

The Carlisles, our neighbors, had two Appaloosas they had bought for their twins. The twins never got terribly fond of the horses or of riding them, so with the twins off to college, the time had arrived to sell the horses or give them away. Janet had contacted the nearby equine veterinarian, who promised to come by that afternoon, which naturally turned into Saturday, four days later. We suspect that equine vets are the rancher's appliance repair person. The vet was not familiar with either of the abandoned horses so her exam was pretty thorough. Nobody had noticed any bad habits either, so Rachel just hopped onto a handy tree stump and then on to the chestnut mare to run her through her paces. The vet gave the horses clean bills of health and offered to put up a sale notice in her office. So it's off to the Carlisles to talk about horses. We wore bright, happy smiles that concealed our conviction that we'd never get through to Mr. C. But we had to try. Should we send Rachel? Hmmmmm. No, she'll be busy telling our students about the corral they needed to build. William was not nearly as disagreeable as we expected and when we offered to pay for the feed (which should be very reasonable given the size of the healthy pasture), construction of the corral, and half of the vet bills, he thought it was a keen idea. In what must have been a moment of dementia, he offered to give us all of the tack they had accumulated. Which we accepted without hesitation. And sent word to our student corral builders that we needed a tack room too. Rachel was oddly quiet, but then, unable to maintain silence, she exploded with a list out of nowhere of the attributes of the mare, insisting that she did not want to get rid of it. We were taken completely by surprise by the passion of her reaction. She retreated into silence again, no doubt mulling over the mare's detributes. And again launched into the subject of horses. "No way," Rachel opened. "We can't keep the mare any longer than it takes to sell her." What? Rachel's lips were moving, but a stranger was doing the talking. Finally, a simple declarative sentence. "She bit me," Rachel announced, baring her shoulder. "Oh, dear," I contributed. It was definitely there. Janet offered to have some acupuncture done on the horse and to work with her one-on-one to see if we could break her of the biting. In the meantime, she should be off limits. At least it wouldn't be hard to remember the names we gave them: Nip and Tuck. The other two horses, the ones bought for the twins, undoubtedly had perfectly good names, but we decided they should begin anew. We might even book those names based solely on their brevity. The Appy mare with a mostly red coat was to be Lucy, of course. And the handsome guy with the eye patch got to be Ricky.

On our way back to Madrigal we patted ourselves on the back and broke into a pathetic rendition of Home On The Range followed by an even worse Streets of Laredo. Plain old city girl to seasoned ranch hand overnight. We'd be able to offer horseback riding to our guests and play horsewomen ourselves. Little did we know how expensive free could be. Oh, well. We took the easy way out of a serious problem: we just threw some money at it and voila! guess what happened. It rode away!

Every now and then I think I see in Michael's eyes a flicker of life as he wonders what's new on the other side of the planet. He gets courted by lots of prestige producing operations, but smoothly shows them out the other door. There was one producer, more obstinate than most, who made a kind of oblique pass at us to see if we were interested in hosting a cooking show on the local cable channel and our reaction was a unanimous, resounding, "No!"

The bocce ball court is in almost constant use since we created and funded The Madrigal International Invitational All Weather Bocce Ball Tournament. We had four tournaments a year, each beginning on the first day of the "season" and, so we didn't forget, ending with the trophy presentation about a week into the next season. By the time the first trophy was presented, the core players had formed teams, set dates and times, and created a self-sustaining fundraising operation for our team.

As luck would have it, because it certainly was not business acumen, Madrigal's finances were excellent. Guests are happy enough that an astonishing fifty per cent of them book for a future visit before they leave. The dining room rarely has less than one full turn on weekends. And our picnics had indeed earned mention in several credible slick magazines. After all, how many picnics feature Quail Breasts Glacé on a bed of wild rice with a hint of truffles? A basket importer worked with Monica and Michael to design a signature basket which turned out to be so popular that we had to limit its availability to guests who bought our picnic package, at least until we got a grip on how many to order and when. Our accountant advised us, with a straight face, to keep operating as if we knew what we were doing. Much to our delight, the biggest profit center after only a year was the dining room. Looking out at the night sky and its generous blanket of stars, there was little evidence of a community big enough to support a gourmet restaurant, but support it they did. I think it was a direct result of having maintained a monthly pot luck fashioned after our bizarre opening night. Anyone who was at Madrigal that evening will remember it as a night of barely controlled mayhem with an underlayment of hysteria. Even now, the suites are reserved according to the Pot Luck schedule. Reservations are mandatory and it is always Standing Room Only. Michael does the planning, staff serve as assistants, and the guests shine with pleasure. And lo and behold!

Halfway through the second bocce ball season there was clearly a good reason to get some kind of seating out there before they took all of the antique chairs out to the game. The bocce gang had found two small but very serviceable grandstand seating units on Craig's List. They didn't discuss or even mention it to us (bad thing), but before moving the stands into place in our pasture they completely refurbished and painted them. As far as players go, one of the very few bona fide rules mandated that overnight guests have first shot at getting a spot in the bocce line-up.

One nice thing about bocce ball is the fact that gender makes no difference to the outcome. While it is possible that traits more often associated with males like impatience or throwing the p-ball with too much muscle, might work in favor of women, that certainly hasn't been the case at Madrigal. You can throw under-handed or over-handed, or you can lob it or, in case of emergency, you can throw it like a girl. Sometimes it works.

Or you can switch to croquet. The only thing that bocce and croquet have in common is the little, hard ball. Bocce is an "each man for himself" free-for-all kind of sport, while croquet is supported by a great deal of structure and science and difficult to absorb rules. The audience at a bocce game is expected to let the world know what is happening by yelling at the players, the officials (if any happen to be there) and anyone else who might care. At a croquet match, the audience respectfully applauds the players in a rather muted manner, much like tennis of old: refined, almost hushed appreciation. They even still have a dress code. It's a game of finesse and its devotees think Madrigal bocce is barbaric. Let 'em.

15 The No Zone

After years of volunteer observation and bypassing some of the driest research materials, I am fully convinced that The No Zone is a viable phenomenon. Most people are aware of The No Zone but are unable to verbalize it. In simplest terms, there appears to be a malfunction or a disturbance in the magnetic field that surrounds mostly men at a height of about twenty-nine inches from the floor, preventing them from being able to see anything below twenty-nine inches from the ground. This can be a handy disability if, for example, you are wrapping gifts or just hiding things from a male. Just put what you want to hide on a shelf no higher than twenty-nine inches. He will walk into the room or area to which he has been directed, give the area a cursory scan, take half a step backwards, repeat the scan cocking his head like a pup, and declare the area clean without having noticed the crumpled car door on the table. This Zone has its origins in early childhood at the moment a child discovers the fun he can have just playing with his external equipment. That's also the point at which the big person in his life says no to all that fun. Hence, The No Zone. Somewhere along the line, the males have restored interest in The No Zone and, now that modesty is apparently not an issue, they are constantly adjusting themselves as if they might have left them at home on the bedside table or a robbery was about to occur. Just imagine if they were easily detachable.

As long as we've all known each other, there seems to be no limit to how artfully we can surprise each other. Monica, for example, is a great fan of dogs in general and especially Golden Retrievers. Big dogs. Real dogs. So you can imagine our surprise when she came home with a cat, and a Siamese at that! He was so picky that he refused to eat anything but peanut butter for brunch and albacore for dinner. We think he won Monica's heart by being convinced that he was really a Siamese dog.

We had not given much thought to the question of pets, even though we all have them. Probably because that kind of discussion is pretty close to making up the rules we seem so averse to crafting. Why is it that just the mention of rules makes us uneasy? Could it be that we know there will be a certain amount of disagreement when we start messing with each other's freedoms? Or that we really do want to be the grownups? Or is it that we know we would choose to break the rules if there were any? I happen to have a black Lab who has slept in her kennel every night of her life and loves it. So I'm thinking we could require that pets be kenneled and I might as well have proposed that pet owners tar and feather their beloved pets.

In my defense, I did ask for options and got not one. I was definitely surprised that no one suggested building a barn with all the proper fittings for spoiled pets. In an effort to take on an easier subject, we agreed that no pet should be left at Madrigal without its owner. Not even for the time it takes to take a short stroll. We could, I suppose, not allow pets at all. Or, if asked, say something like "Pets not encouraged." And it would have to be enforced for all pets, even the tampon look-a-likes, no matter how well trained.

The biggest problem with pets as guests at Madrigal is that Madrigal is designed to minimize the guests' responsibilities and maximize the guests' opportunities to get away from things that dog and cat owners find so adorable about their pets, like begging for treats, jumping onto laps, bringing you toys to play with, rubbing against your legs, slopping water all over the floor, barking, using the house as a restroom, or bringing laundry into the living room. And there are plenty of other reasons to leave your pets at home. If you absolutely must bring your shedding, flea-bitten highly pedigreed animal on vacation with you, bring a portable kennel with you for starters. Okay, that might be a little strong. Then, if we haven't already done so, we can refer you to one of three boarding kennels in town, all of which offer a much reduced rate for our guests. If you want to check them out online, the two kennels that take only dogs are vintnerskennels.com and caninecastle.com. The kennel that only takes cats is thecathouse.com. Naturally.

Ever since our inaugural evening, the subject of space has crept into our minds with enough insistence that we found ourselves actually considering adding on a bedroom/ office. One evening when we were all at Madrigal, we started several serious discussions and concluded that what we really needed was a vacation from thinking. If we want a one-day turnaround, we could check out history and art in Monterey, shopping and strolling in Carmel, wine tasting in Cambria, or lazing in the sun at Mussel Shoals. If we can stretch to two nights and three days, we expand our options by a bundle. Then we could take in a play at the Geffen Theater, spend the night at one of the chi chi hotels and spend the next day shopping in Pasadena. For that matter, we could choose from casinos, county fairs, or camping (don't panic; that would be catered camping). And there's always Monica's country estate, Rio Dulce Ranch, or Catherine's offspring with their fully restored Brown & Brown house in San Diego, or their other home in Magdaleña Ranch. This kind of decision requires time and a sobering amount of planning. So, within the span of about fifteen minutes, we were set to go to Monterey. We rented a huge, luxurious van, which is plenty roomy for six people and their purchases. We got reservations for adjoining rooms at The Highlands Inn thanks to Monica's fancy contacts. Then, and only then, did we remember that we have a business to maintain. The responsibility for Madrigal had never been clearer. Or more soundly resented. None of us could imagine that Madrigal would be a hindrance to our fun. So we spent the next hour playing devil's advocate to each other's suggestions and decided to take the now-traditional path to problem solving: throw money at it. We called Michael, Dorothy and Socorro into the library and laid out our plans and concerns. They looked at each other. They looked at us. They looked back at each other and said, almost simultaneously, "What do you think we've been doing when you go home? Having one of you here at all times doesn't mean that each of you is equally competent in all parts of the operation." Whatever that meant. We did get the basic points, all of which were connected to our authorization to spend money and sign checks. With just a small raise, they would take on the responsibility of managing Madrigal together Sunday through Thursday. In any significant disagreements, if we were to be unreachable by phone, Michael's opinions were to prevail. The personalities made it a little dicey but we felt good about it. And they had enough contacts in the valley to make it through virtually any crisis. And we had enough cellphones (some of which have live batteries) to sink a ship. Knock on wood.

Off we went into the wild blue yonder, feeling quite smug about our quick getaway when Liz asked if anyone had brought her huuuge Vera Bradley bag. Cursory shuffle search around the back of the van. More thorough search including groceries. The next stage of the search always involves getting someone to unhook the seat belt and stretch as far back as possible, but still revealing lacy underthings. The next phase requires pulling off the freeway and conducting a proper search. Turns out the bag is not in the van. What to do? Go back? Do without? At least locate the bag and pick it up later? Nah. We'll just hope some nice person finds it and calls the rightful owner. Everything goes back into the van, stuffed into every nook when Catherine makes a little tiny squeaking sound and points to the front passenger floorboard and the Vera Bradley bag. Oh. Look under there, too? A classic case of cross-gender affliction if I ever heard one. Back into the van, everybody very relieved and impressed with Liz's apparent calm. And still on point for the coast. Monica drew the short straw and had to do the driving until 3:00 shift change when Catherine would take over. At least Catherine had driven a van before; Monica had owned and driven only sexy little cars for the last several years, so her time at the wheel was very exciting. First we sang a bit, mostly to assure ourselves that although we would very likely not live through lunch we'd be together. We stopped at every little souvenir shop, looking for heaven knows what, but each stop took us closer to a change in drivers and a game of musical chairs. Monica is not a bad driver; she just turns and swerves unexpectedly. At one intersection, for example, four cars were aggressively trying to be in the same place all at once so Monica took the Biggest Car option and won handily. But she acted so suddenly that some epithet about snorting pigs, accompanied by pig snorting and squealing, took over her normally genteel speech patterns and had us all convulsed in tears of laughter. Even today. If one of us makes that snorting pig sound we cannot maintain any sort of decorum. That trip will forever be remembered as the Pig Trip. Not what you hope for in an image, but certainly accurate.

After a good night's sleep, largely credited to the

very pricey wine Liz selected to accompany our equally wonderful dinner, we headed out on foot to watch the creditcardnivores. Every VSOP (Very Special and Over Priced) designer is represented among the shops on the hilly cobblestone streets. Faced with clearance sale after clearance sale of silk blouses costing $275, camisoles on sale for $200, and pet accessories like collars with real gemstones costing well into the $600 range, I am not tempted. Mind you, I love the occasional frivolity, but this kind of excess is like puppies and peanut butter: a pairing destined for disaster. As much as we love Madrigal, the decision to have a vacation elsewhere was nothing short of brilliant. We picked up some great menu and service ideas as well as suppliers. One small thing we hadn't thought of was a nicely framed chalkboard with contemporary information for guests, including time of sunrise and sunset, times of upcoming bocce matches and other amusements and activities. All in all, I think we would choose Monterey for shopping and the DrugMart Superstore for buying.

As a group, we have collected a sizeable store of wisdom, along with the need to share it in the form of learned advice to friends, acquaintances, family and complete strangers. It does not need to be verified. It doesn't even need to be true. But having one or two successes in giving extraneous advice goes a long way toward establishing your fallibility quotient. If our advice is accepted, it may or may not become lore. That means we must be ever alert to new opportunities for sharing our wisdom with the rest of the known world. This occasionally results in our being late because, truth be told, we were scared to death that some major catastrophe so horrendous that no one was willing to tell us on the phone had befallen our slice of paradise. Obviously texting was out of the question because it hadn't yet been invented and captured our hearts and minds. It was much like the first time you leave your infant with a babysitter, even if the sitter is the baby's grandmother. So we continued to drive at a snail's pace, getting quieter by the mile until we turned the corner, parked, and piled out of the van like teenage girls coming home from summer camp. Once inside, Madrigal just briefly scolded us by putting all of the lights out in the dining room. No panic. Just bring out the rest of the candles. We tossed our purchases, which we had vowed not to make, into the library, gave little trinkets to the staff, which we had vowed not to do, and sat down to a delicious short rib dinner.

After dinner, we called sweet, kindhearted Dorothy into the library for what is now called a "Nightcap Recap" of her weekend as Assistant Manager. Dorothy was so nervous about being in the library with the six of us that we felt compelled to give her a glass of one of the Port sisters, Tawny or Ruby. When Liz picked up the bottle she couldn't help but notice that the rich color was a bit faded and the bottle was quite light. What do you do? Do you call her out for a minor infraction we've all committed at one time or another? Only if you want to risk losing her out of embarrassment. Do you completely ignore it? If you want to appear to be a soft touch and a little stupid. Liz took the high road and simply poured her a glass but made a small show of holding the glass up to the light after the pour. Nobody missed it. Such a simple lesson for all of us: decant the expensive spirits like Midleton into the tantalus and assume that Michael will be around with the key whenever we need it. Such a situation is very likely the only reason that gin and vodka are staples in liquor cabinets. It is certainly more difficult to tell how much has been filched when it looks like water from day one.

16 The Flash Flood

Everyone has speed bumps along the road to maturity, and many of those bumps herald mid-life changes that can be bothersome to some, cumbersome to others and perfectly hilarious to those who haven't been there yet. Even just for a visit. We call them speed bumps for lack of a more descriptive term. They serve one purpose and one purpose only: to make our journeys as unpredictable as possible. The speed bumps are not evenly spaced or of consistent heights. They could be invisible lead rocks of varying sizes. They are the weights that prevent us from getting rid of the junk that hides in the carefully packed under-bed box of cardigan sweaters that you meticulously folded with lots and lots of tissue paper but haven't worn for years, or at least since high school. Something happens as the distance between the bumps is reduced, making it impossible to free yourself from them. Try to get rid of chafing dishes, fondue forks and ashtrays. Can't be done. The minute a chafing dish appears on your horizon, you begin to dream of more sophisticated times. Hot hors d'oeuvres. Dinner parties using recipes from the top chefs in the south of France. Accompanied by weird vegetables with absolutely no flavor. You might even buy a used chafing dish at the thrift store thinking that there will be an opportunity to use it. Of course you can use it. You can plant precious plants in it. Or you can store your granddaughter's rock and shell collection in it. Or you can spend days polishing the copper and then use it as a very upscale dog dish. Resist. Then try to get fewer than three pieces of junk mail in one day. I have finally put the wastebasket within an arm's distance to the mailbox so that I don't get bogged down in circulars for unnecessary stuff on my way to somewhere else. You have a fairly reliable clue that they don't have a firm grip on their direct mail program when you receive your renewal offer the same day you get the card which declares you paid in full for five more years. They must be competing with the garage door installation people for most unnecessary mailbox debris.

Actually, there may be clues along the way that would forewarn us, giving us an opportunity, albeit slim, to slip around some of these speed bumps entirely. We all battle the subtle but insidious weight gain that occurs mostly after the children have moved out, which made it unnecessary to set any kind of example for them. Then, one member of the household goes on a diet. One of the basic laws of physics that got drummed into our fragile teenage brains says that matter doesn't just vanish; it relocates. And if you're in close regular contact with someone losing weight, some of that weight will inevitably stick to you. That's why you so often see skinny girls with heavy ones. That keeps the excess matter from sticking to the skinny one. And the skinny ones know this. Skinny women select their friends from a pool of porky ladies, which isn't such a bad idea. The vanishing matter theory does not, however, work exactly the same way on all body parts. Consider the wings, those loose areas on the back of the upper arm that flap like wings when you wave. In some circles, they are called bingo wings, which brings up a visual that would more than do the trick. These wings gather matter very rapidly, much faster than other areas on the body, and they cannot be seen without the help of a mirror or a really, really good friend. The best defense is keeping an eye on your great-aunts for signs of wings in your DNA and then consider exercising them away. After that doesn't work, you'll just need to have the plastic surgeon put you on a regular recall program to keep those wings looking firm and fit.

So there we sat with Dorothy, who became quite animated toward the end of her second drink. In what we thought was an awkward attempt to offer pleasant conversation, she reported with no drama whatsoever that we had a poltergeist in residence and should every now and then check for signs of same. Apparently, they are often confused with packrats: vile, dirty, nasty rodents that steal things from their hosts. Packrats are particularly fond of shiny things like jewelry which, once stolen by a packrat, is not likely to be seen again. "And what," someone finally asked, "should we do about it?" We all did our very best to appear casual while we grilled Dorothy all about the alleged poltergeist and why did Dorothy know so much about her/him anyway? We were happy to subscribe to the belief that they are mischievous but not mean, almost elf-like. Dorothy tried to let it go, but Ruby Port had her by the lips and wouldn't let her change the subject. She paused, considering whether to go on and maybe risk her job for not having said something sooner. With Ruby's help, she opted to dive right back in. "They're never nice," she said. "Sometimes they're funny, but most often that's an accident. They hide things; they break things; they move things; they spill things. And (watch out, she's got a full head of steam) do you guys by any chance have any idea how long it takes in a burg like this to work off one miserable bad moment? I can tell you. It takes two generations. The first stage of your penance will lead you to recognize that the Ladies' Auxiliary is far too influential and has an abundance of volunteer opportunities right up your alley: housekeeping duties in the senior center laundry, reading books they don't want to hear to hyperactive children in the day care center, driving the infirm and incontinent to appointments. Plenty to keep you busy while you're not working very much." Although the critters obviously have believers here, we weren't among them. We asked Dorothy to keep an eye out for any signs of poltergeists and let us know if there are any sightings. The more interesting bit of conversation was the existence of the Ladies' Auxiliary. They sound like a group we should know and avoid. A little like packrats.

When you've paid your community dues, according to the Auxiliary Board, your child or children will take the baton and, with luck, make it through high school without a pregnancy or lots of drugs. Then, after you have fully repaid the gossip mill, when someone refers to the dyed black hair incident, most locals will just give a dismissive wave of the hand and say something like, "She must be one tough cookie, that Dorothy. You notice that polter-whatever has never been back." "Oh, no," she thought, "If they only knew. Dorothy spent several sleepless nights trying to determine where her responsibility began and ended. Maybe she should just keep her head down and continue to please her bosses. Maybe she should take her chances with being up front. She had not, after all, seen the poltergeist or any sign of it for close to two years, and before that, it was six years. But, come to think of it, there had been a few little incidents recently that could have been warnings. There was the honey pot with no lid that tipped over in the cabinet, emptying its contents on the shelf it belonged on and the shelves beneath it. Or the unplugged refrigerator which, thank heavens, has an alarm. Or, just maybe, the down comforter that refused to stay on the bed. No matter what the owner suggested. Dorothy decided to take the less complicated road and say nothing, or at least say nothing unless or until the poltergeist started to be destructive. Dorothy had read somewhere that spirits can be neutralized by being named. She loved her job and if keeping it meant whispering names into closets and cupboards in search of the right name, that was a small price to pay. So what if people thought she was a little odd? She would protect Madrigal and herself as fiercely as she could. She would even, she admitted, protect and fight for Rachel, despite the delicate aspects of their relationship.

One of Dorothy's finds when she was scouting for a name for the poltergeist was a basket with at least fifty pairs of reading glasses in it. Clever us: they were to be in the dining room so that they were accessible without attracting attention. Not so clever us: we forgot all about them. Then, after Dorothy resurrected them, they got as far as the reception desk, which turned out to be a perfect location. In they came; out they went. Just as if we had planned it, and guests made no pretense about taking them. The occasional Catholic, needing to anticipate a bit of guilt, sometimes mumbled something like, "I'll bring these right back," with no intention of doing so. We considered that maybe a little white lie was easier to confess than petty thievery. The love/hate relationship we have with reading glasses is almost consuming. For one thing, most of them do not have the strength stamped or engraved on them. That would enable wearers to identify or narrow the field of ownership rather than have this perpetual exchange cluster. When we purchase our first pair of reading glasses, it isn't all that bad. They are invariably very fashionable and small enough to be invisible if you like. And some are downright whimsical. Their attractiveness, however, is reduced exponentially by the wearer's actual need for them. By the time you simply cannot read a menu or, worse, the information that comes with your hormone-balancing prescriptions, you learn to hate them, resisting your dependence on them with all the waning focus you can muster. I theorize that it is not a vision problem. It is simply a problem of light. If the light is bright enough, you can read anything. Except maybe street signs at night.

Our little trip to Monterey gave us a tremendous dose of confidence in our ability to travel together. As a result, we didn't wait twenty-four hours before starting to plan the next journey. The question of the day was: should spouses and significant others be included in the next long journey? Considering the fact that three of the six of us have husbands, you'd think their inclusion would be a slam dunk. Far from it. We started planning the trip such that the girls would see Paris together and meet up with our men for the second half of the journey in the south of France. Now let's look at this seedling of a plan. We do the Dorothy Parker in Paris stuff, like slouching on metal café chairs à la Melina Mercouri and wearing hats as though we had dozens of them, and reminiscing about literature and such great films as Last Year At Marienbad and Phaedra at the beginning without our men, and then reward them for being so amenable by taking them on a driving tour of The Lavender Trail. I can't even pretend that my husband would prefer side trips planned and outfitted by someone else, featuring picnic baskets filled with bread and cheese, fresh fruit and plenty of wine. His usual refrain: "A twist of lemon please. NO lime," mostly would have failed for lack of tequila. Some people just have a limit on beauty they can absorb. And some just think they do. The biggest problem, after finding two weeks we could all be out of our respective offices at the same time, was how to ensure that our two (or maybe three) men would be entertained and still not be underfoot. By the same token, how much Eiffel Tower, Louvre, Arc de Triomphe, Sacré Coeur and Notre Dame can anyone take in before they actually become their fantasies about Paris and its inhabitants? Any of us was likely to be extremely susceptible to falling helplessly in love with Paris, but it seemed to hit Liz the fastest and the hardest. Practically the moment we deplaned, Liz took wine critiquing to new heights. We were especially impressed with her command of the Language of The Grape, which consists of fewer than twenty words used in a multitude of combinations to describe the countless varietals. Part of it is that it seems easier to just follow along knowing that the reason the Language of the Grape is difficult to learn is that the people who make the wine and those who sell the wine don't really want you to understand that, dollar for dollar, tequila can get you there faster and cheaper every time. One of the few downsides of spirits is that there's nothing to talk about unless we include martinis and really, really old single malt whisky. It's far easier, certainly in France, to immerse yourself in the mystique of The Grape, listening to the litany of The Grape qualities, repetition of woody, oaky, bouquet ad nauseam. I always think it might be fun to have a few retorts handy so that one could say things like, "You can almost taste the raisins in the finish. Is it a breakfast wine?" or "This red is quite dry for its age. Could that be why it's so leggy?" or "It has great legs but the skirt is a bit short," or "Ooooh, check out the nose on this one! It's had plenty of work done." The wine on arrival was a great idea, but our apartment was so wonderful that we nearly forgot to go to dinner on our first night there. Of course we had forgotten that dinner starts at ten or even eleven in the really snazzy places.

Our apartment was on the fourth floor of a four hundred-year-old converted monastery on the West Bank overlooking the Seine and the Louvre. Incredible. We were so filled with the culture that is Paris that we gathered in a beautiful chapel and sang a round of Amazing Grace in honor of an ill friend and some other travelers joined us saying they came in because they thought they had heard angels singing. They were right.

Wine has most certainly occupied the top position among worlds of tradition since its first ceremonial bottling in the halls of Montezuma and the Chambers of Cleopatra. Historians have found shards of wine bottles in archaeological digs around the world, leading them to profess that wine has been fundamental to the betterment of civilization since time began. Because this philosophy has been so long accepted as fact by oenophiles and people in the garden furnishing industries, no recent studies have been conducted to re-test the validity of this position. And anyway, it's more important to know what you like than what Joe Schmo likes. (Unless Joe is particularly handsome and extraordinarily wealthy.)

The reader may have noticed that husbands were not, after all, encouraged to join us. Not quite true:

Catherine's husband met her in Avignon for the last two nights of the trip. The three remaining spouses had excellent excuses and they may or may not remember that days like those go in the vacation book as unexcused absences.

Perhaps the most memorable sights in all of France were Monet's gardens and the profusion of water lilies. The air was redolent with the scent of beauty just as enchanting as it was when Monet strolled through his gardens. Liz could have lost herself there. And, just short of that, she could have lost herself in Willis Wine Bar where the food was so flawless and the presentation such a work of art that she photographed it from all angles, much to Alex's dismay.

Travel lacks something if you make the itinerary too ambitious or completely inflexible. It could be daring that it lacks, or a sense of opportunity, or even a sense of silly. Whatever it indicates, these women have definitely embraced the spur of the moment concept of travel. Who else would "stop by" Cannes in complete innocent ignorance of the fact that we were there right smack dab in the middle of the Cannes Film Festival, covered with mud, lost, low on fuel, with no lodging in Cannes and all of our worldly possessions back where we started on this overcast, slightly dreary day? No worries. We have Rachel behind the wheel. As the misty sky turned into drizzle, Rachel advised her passengers that one little whine from anybody would land the whiner in the driver's seat. And then came the rain. Real rain. Rain straight out of a faucet. Torrential rain. We were very, very quiet. And then came the flash flood, which sent our buggy up the berm and nearly off the road. Nice people that we are, we pulled over to let a wonderful old truck pass and he repaid us by covering our car with a thick layer of mud. Large wet leaves go a long way toward cleaning the car, but chamois they were not. All told, it took two adult men, three teenage boys and three teenage girls to get enough mud off the windows to make the car drivable. The scene reminded me so much of the Madrigal kids that it made me terribly homesick. All I could think of was my Craftsman Suite and a luxurious soak in the tub, until the steamy water started to cool. But for the time being, I was grateful for Rachel and her legendary driving skills.

17 Worries

The arrival at home was very different from our return from Monterey. Not bad, just different. We were anxious to share our stories with our Madrigal family as well as our own families, and we were genuinely glad to be home.

Lest anyone think that our menfolk were neglected in our arrival home, be assured that they were not. We arrived at Madrigal at about eight o'clock on Friday morning, so we were mostly unpacked, napped and laid back when our Very Significant Other People (Oooohhh! Another VSOP) arrived at eleven thirty or so.

We had closed Madrigal to guests for the weekend of our return (with plenty of notice to our paying guests) and arranged a no-guest weekend, our first, with all staff on duty to make us feel like guests. Before we left on our journey, we created a sensational menu that challenged even Michael. The tantalus was unlocked and placed provocatively on the library table. We had two masseuses, approved by Rachel, on call. Actually, Rachel wanted to treat all of us, but we voted her down on that dumb idea.

We hadn't worried as hard on this trip, mostly because we did stay in touch thanks to the internet, which proved sensational for our purposes. We utilized some of our travel time to do a little meaningful, objective soul searching so we also had a better handle on what our priorities should be. First, we needed to outfit Rachel's Treatment Room, especially the perishables like treatment creams and ointments, supplements, and equipment. Our message to Rachel: we set up that treatment room to be beautiful and functional. Now go do it. And get your upstairs suite finished at the same time.

Oddly enough, that was all it took to break the impasse she was having with herself. Rachel isn't inclined to procrastinate, but she is a little scattered at times. By the time our plane hit the tarmac, Rachel was armed with sketches, pages from a dozen magazines and five articles on holistic practices. Within a week, she had the Harmony Suite and her One World Suite outfitted so thoroughly that when Sylvia, the owner of a nearby massage competitor, "stopped by" to say hello, nobody batted an eye and she made very short work of her visit. Somebody heard her say, "No way. This a different deal entirely." You've got that right, Cookie. Her cursory look-see was the best thing she could have done for us, aside from saying unflattering things that made her sound just plain uninformed.

Not one to let an opportunity slip by unnoticed, as soon as Sylvia left, Rachel grabbed a fistful of fresh lavender, put it in a vase and hot-footed it over to Total

Wellness to make a reciprocal nice-nice with Sylvia. Given an alternative, Sylvia's customers would flee for their lives. And they did. Rachel promised not to raid Sylvia's client list and offered to pay her the equivalent of one visit for every customer who decided to take his or her business from Total Wellness to Harmony. Within three months, Sylvia had moved her practice into her home, which inspired Alex to offer her financial help for beauty school. Fortunately, Sylvia turned her down before we had a chance to tell Alex not to be so generous with other people's money. The situation inspired Alex to make a rather sentimental toast to which we raised our glasses to them as likes us 'n' them as don't. And anyway, where would we put somebody else? Space seemed to diminish every day. We had lots of conversation about adding another building to our holdings, and we decided to explore the possibilities seriously. The first thing we learned is that the city is not at all in favor of making room for more people and emphasizes that fact with archaic housing regulations. So why not put up pre-fab housing? That's even harder to do here. Okay then, how about movable housing? We let the word germinate for a couple of weeks and then ran a classified ad in the local weekly paper. Wow. There are lots of people who have bought the top of the line motor home only to find that they hated being upper crust gypsies, living first class on the road. For that kind of money they could spend time at the Ritz Carlton. Then we have the issues of specific uses, size and amenities. And which are the best of the bunch? All of our research made it patently clear that the most attractive, durable addition to Madrigal was going to be a motor home. God forbid that anyone in our lives, past or present, should hear that we had fallen on such tragic times that we were living in a motor home. With just one more infusion of ReadyCash, we could buy a Winnebago, camouflage it with siding to match the house, outfit it with three offices, decide our plans were flawed and start over with two offices and a big TBD (To Be Determined).

All but Alex thought it was a terrific idea, but Alex, for some reason unknown to any of us, went nuts. "What is your problem?" she asked the group at large. "Yes, I grew up in Bakersfield, but that doesn't make me a bad person. The climb may be a little steeper when you don't start as high up the mountain as some of us have. As a matter of fact, I think that makes me a better person. At least the friends I have there are true friends." We were dumbfounded by her outburst. The timing, the content, the rancor. All of it was wrong. Liz took the proverbial bull by the proverbial horns and followed Alex up to her suite, leaving Catherine in tears, Rachel and Monica looking for something that might help and me wondering if I should write it all down so that I can include it in the chronicles. We hadn't really had very many disputes, but the few we did have were humdingers because we know each other so well. And we knew without a doubt that this one would be of epic proportions when Liz lowered her already commanding voice and said, simply, "Theodora Louise, knock that off." The door closed with quiet authority and we all stayed clear of the zone.

In fact, we knew Alex would benefit from a day trip to some shopping mecca. The problem lay in the fact that nobody else really wanted to leave Madrigal yet. During cocktails, we proposed that somebody head to the outlet stores to the north and find an appropriate gift for Michael's birthday. By process of elimination, Monica and Alex got the nod. Long drive, but it promised to be fruitful. Not to worry.

Worries occur to fill the spaces left by problems. For instance, we were having a little problem keeping the area around the front steps looking deliberate. And of course the solution presented itself. Most herbs are a bit raggedy looking when they start. So if we planted some deliberates, like a few azaleas and some lush, low growing ferns, the garden would have anchors. Problem solved. Except for the sword ferns somebody slipped in on us. But they'd be easy to worry about. With that problem solved, we could worry about several things. First, when will we have some annuals for arrangements in the house? We had not even discussed having flowers in the house and it had already become a problem. No, I think it's just a worry. Maybe problems come with solutions and worries just congregate to attract attention. One last thought on the subject: do you suppose that you get more points if you can say I'm worried about this problem?

Bert, wonderful Bert, went traipsing through storage lots finding the biggest and best looking motor homes around. He also put together a plan for co-ownership. The titled owner would essentially rent the motor home to us for ten or eleven months for use as office space. He had noticed a For Sale sign on a colossal Winnebago, far more commodious than the nice tech-y looking Airstream, or the Fleetwood with the worst color combinations yet. As hard as we tried, none of us could refrain from giving Alex just a tiny touch of a bad time about being from Bakersfield and having an office in a vehicle, suggesting that she would of course be our resident expert. Her withering look was sufficiently forceful that we backed away quickly hoping to circumvent a replay of Alex's unleashed furies. Morning had brought an abatement of her unprecedented anger, but it had certainly left some residue. She would only say that if we were ever to grow up, we would understand. None of us, even Alex, would promote the general concept of growing up, and there was no show of hands by volunteers willing to take a shot on the other side. So we learned to live with the mystery that was Alex's fury.

18 Hair, Shoes and Bras

Our wins at Madrigal fueled our fires for innovation. They did not make us cautious, but rather curious. Our successes were compelling enough that we had feature articles in national publications under such subject headings as gourmet foods and picnics, entertaining guests you've never met, weather and parties.

The biggest problems generated by our evidently good ideas were in not knowing when to quit and how to stay focused. We needed to spend some time at a revised drawing board, sorting through our existing programs and operations and ideas that were just spilling out. Our inventory was remarkably creative and noteworthy. Surveying our landscape from the widow's walk and viewing it clockwise you could see our charming gate in the picket fence, and the sunny side of the herb garden, which turned out to be a big plus because when our students discovered that partial sun is a lot of nonsense, the garden flourished. Sun. Shade. Pick one. Or don't. Continuing around, we could see a place for the Winnebago, just past the croquet court decorated with colorful pansies. Next

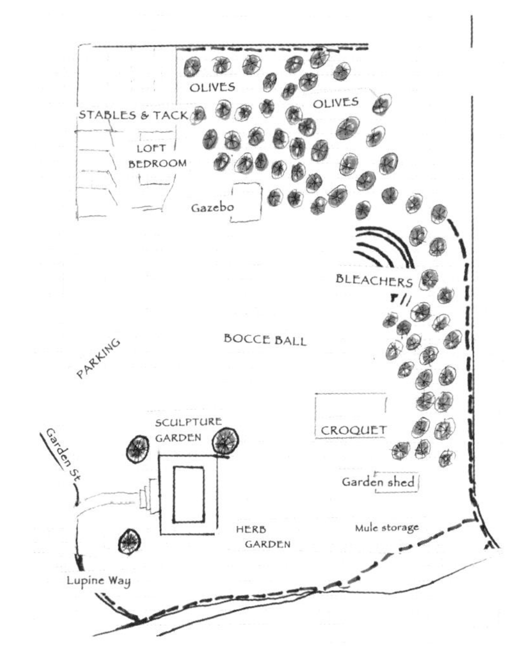

came the barn and tack room and the bleachers originally restored by our students and put in place by bocce fans. The bocce contingent stayed strong and competitive.

There are as many kinds of "coachmen" as there are people who drive them. At the showoff end of the scale we have the Winnebago, which is Michigan for "I wanna be gone!" – a little refrain heard in almost every motor home as the snowbird driver heads for Florida – and at the other end of the luxury spectrum are the resale fifth wheels. Still considering the low end as a possibility for storage at Madrigal, we admitted among ourselves that we had more research to do in that department. For one thing, people who choose the resale fifth wheel route are often scorned, even by their brethren with awnings, bike racks and other decorative items like custom spare tire covers. There also seems to be a link between purging unloved possessions from your garage and moving them several times before abandoning the disposal mission altogether. Back into their crannies. The Unwanted. This type of arrangement, mostly storage, has brought back the word purgatory as in a place to store things you don't even remember owning. It's different from Limbo, another vacation site wiped out by Vatican II. The basic difference between the two is that Limbo is for people left out accidentally and Purgatory is where you go for short term punishment, much like being sent to the library with nothing to read. These clusters of lots, most called mobile home parks, have enormous political clout and very expensive attorneys. Otherwise, why would sensible people turn out in droves to vote the mobile home ballot and candidates shuffle and curtsy in hopes of getting that vote? While there are dozens of incarnations of these clusters of movable homes, called variably mobile home parks, mobile home estates, and trailer parks, we knew that first we needed to determine use or uses of The Monster.

On weekends, several youngsters from nearby farms bring produce and a pitiful selection of fresh flowers to the makeshift corner market and produce stand near the house. They did have enough variety that would please our flower fans. But how to get it done? We were more than busy before this project hit us. Ah hah! Little Socorro. For some reason we rarely thought of Socorro when odd projects came to mind. It might be that she was hardly more than a child herself. When she left her family's home, she found a job as a nanny with a wonderful family and stayed until her mother was certain that the job she had been offered at Madrigal was secure and would get her an education. As a result, Socorro can do pretty much anything. We handed her the keys to our very macho farm truck, and sent her off to do our bidding. She grabbed onto the task like a lifeline and when she returned, she politely asked if she could surprise us, which meant she'd like to be alone. And hot dog! Another star was born. In less than an hour, Socorro created three masterpieces with local flowers, vegetables and fruits. “Absolutely fabulous” was Michael’s assessment. She suggested that we have flowers on the piano at all times, an arrangement of flowers and produce combined in the dining room, and a smaller bouquet at the desk. We listened politely for as long as we could and finally interrupted ourselves to tell her that she was now our official Florista. She was beside herself with that pure, effervescent joy we lose access to about the time we gain the ability to curl our lip at a parent. When we told her that we would order her a chambray shirt with her name and title on it, she nearly hyperventilated. But her wise mother quickly reminded her that she didn’t wear clothing with her name on it because it makes it too easy for a stranger to act like a friend. What a wonderful decision! We didn’t really reduce Socorro’s workload, but we did allow her to bring her daughter in to help with changing linens when she felt it was necessary. There is certainly more to that story and it undoubtedly involves a young male with good eyes, a full testosterone load, a great self image and a high level of optimism. Angel was blessed and cursed with head-spinning beauty, and she had not a single clue that she was in any way different from her pals in the sixth grade. The adults in her life had no trouble understanding the concept of a highly supervised adolescence. But the boys were definitely sniffing around. Socorro, on the other hand, was not a raving beauty, but she had been a loving, dedicated mother since Angel was born just a week after her own fifteenth birthday.

Socorro’s memories and the implications of those loneliest of days are never far below the surface. Shortly after Angel was born, Socorro’s stepfather commanded each of the nine family members seated at the dinner table to stand and give a brief definition of “family” one at a time. They each defined family, very carefully, and then were permitted to sit. Socorro, trying to settle her new baby, was the last left standing when her stepfather snarled at her: "Don't bother, Socorro. You have already turned your back on this family. You may be excused now to gather up what belongings you can carry and leave this house for the rest of your life. You'll get nothing from the people you know inside or outside the family because I have assured them it would be foolish to get involved." Abruptly, Socorro's mother stood with fire in her eyes, slapped the heavy wood table, made a sound much like a hungry bear waking from a winter's sleep and said, through gritted teeth, barely loud enough for all to hear, "This is MY home, built by my father and my brother for our family. You no longer have a place here. You will never again defile it with such cruelty and bile as you have spent tonight. You, amigo del diablo, who has so little to give you value, may go away from here and discover that you are not a friend to anyone, not even to yourself. The enemy is not hiding from us. The enemy is right here," smashing a china bowl onto the floor just for emphasis. "That knife you carry cannot protect you from the fates, who are seeking you as we speak." As if in a dream, Socorro's mother walked to the head of the table, picked up the knife and stood stock-still, drawing herself up to her full four feet nine as she summoned all of her strength to slap his cheek as hard as she could. "Now get OUT!" As you can imagine, the story has been re-told dozens of times. Her brothers were there for the whole show, but rarely talk about it. Could be a trace of guilt, methinks. Whatever the version, they all include a knife and a slap. And his departure. Nobody misses him. Nobody. Needless to say, Socorro and Angel instantly became living legends...personalities young women (and not-so-young ones) could look to for inspiration in every corner of their lives.

Some of the most important lessons you learn refurbishing a house are skilfully hidden from you until such time as you need them yesterday. They were there. It's just that we weren't paying attention until Liz took a header down the stairs. Suddenly, access for disabled guests became an issue. Not just a toilet seat here and there, but safety bars, stairs, room for a wheelchair. You get the picture. And our star witness is graceful, slim Liz, who inadvertently selected our own house to stage a trip and fall. Fortunately, she "just" sprained an ankle, an injury even the most cavalier doctors admit is one of the slowest and most painful to heal. But there we were, one of our youngest and best with her foot in a walking cast, dragging it around like Quasimodo when she couldn't get away with crutches. She was, however, an excellent guinea pig for our purposes: wheelchair, cast, crutches, cane, walkers, handrails, elevators. You may be relieved to know that it was more than an exercise in hospitality. We were preparing for our own limitations, so we might as well go first class. At least people with the need to lug medical equipment around with them get just plain tired of the task and abandon the reflection in the mirror in favor of stopping to put their charges somewhere. Anywhere. I strongly recommend that you pre-shop for medical supplies and equipment so that you're at least marginally prepared for the contemporary offerings. They're pretty snazzy. Walkers may sport horns with a variety of tunes and at minimum they have seats with pockets for essentials like your cellphone and the little bag of chips you liberated from the dining room. You can buy a cane with a tripod foot that converts to a seat just like proper hunting stools of yore. As expected, retailers handling medical equipment and supplies are faced with an almost impossible task in creating a shopping environment that is light, cheery, welcoming and efficient when their stock in trade is subjects no one wants to think about. For that reason, many shops that carry medical supplies keep them in the back. Imagine spending your day describing the advantages of one potty seat over another and the absorbency of various incontinence products. "Of course, Sir. This discreet little kidney-shaped bowl is perfect with any flatware pattern. And the booster seat has an automatic scent dispenser." Just looking at what they have today does not bode well for what you'll need tomorrow. Liz taught us to ask.

For some reason, we never quite remember clearly what our hair looked like before the steel wool fairy made his midnight foray. On the plus side, the variety of hair colors and treatments on any senior bus has liberated a generation of perfectly average women to play with their hair. They are free to color it, curl it, or even dispense with it altogether. In fact, women are so glib about hair color that they're sneaking into blues, mahogany, orange, various shades of peach, white, and now they're keeping up with the kids with florescent hairspray.

Hair, shoes and bras. Can these possibly be what we're going to focus on in our "golden" years? Not me. Mostly, I intend to not notice any changes in my appearance. And that begins with hair. Just about the time we're recognizing ourselves in mirrors, the steel wool fairy makes another of those visits and voila! The next morning, you wake up with somebody else's hair. No amount of washing it, slathering conditioner on it, beer rinses, vinegar rinses or Alberto V05 (my grandmother's favorite because that's where she stored her whiskey). At this moment in time, your hair is on its own in a cruel double-whammy over which you have no control. Steel wool or not, take a moment to smell the concoction add a layer of texture that can only come from using the littlest pink curlers and a single paper on each to get maximum burn, and then head for the color aisle. We spend hours and hours and piles of money trying to tame the hair beast into submission. And we're generally at least mildly dissatisfied. Then, after all the failed attempts, it simply gives up. You want it brown? You get gray. You want it blonde? Let's try dark gray. You want auburn? You get a dingy gray. You want white? You get yellow. Whatever your choice, you're going to get what your hair wants you to have. Or if it's been curly, you won't be able to make even a semblance of a wave. Surely they don't ask their hair stylists to create a hair-do that has all the characteristics of #00 steel wool. And then again, maybe they do.

Many eighty-ish women have iron clad pacts with best friends to prevent such spectacles from dogging us in public. They vow that they will not let each other be seen in public with steel wool hair or teflon bra straps. The concept is good, but the likelihood for success remains to be seen. Of course the first question is, who is the last to wear a bra? And do they accumulate so that the wearer of the last one is toting the rest of them because they didn't get on board sooner?

We did decide to dispose of our bras. All of them. Because they lie. We are pre-conditioned to detest our bras. Since that magical time in the '60s when we staged a bra-burning for the media and granted ourselves permission to live without them, bras have become increasingly irritating, so we have developed still more new industries designed to support, tether or otherwise glamorize those breasts. They make us look bigger, better, older, more slender, Rubenesque, younger and/or more fit. They do not, however, make us look smarter. But all of the attention paid to these appurtenances leads potential friends and companions to have false expectations. Can you imagine the shock of glimpsing a seventy-year-old breast when the last one you'd seen was a perky thirty years old? Those old ones look just like Nopal cactus: flat, a bit spiny, and pointed directly at the ground. Perhaps it was not the best of ideas but we were just kids and who knew that those lovely curves would outgrow the space allotted them? And let us dispense with the impossible notion perpetrated by unattractive women that somehow manufactured breasts are inferior to originals. That smacks of the same idiotic reverse snobbery that would have you believe that an automobile is an automobile. Your crappy faded red Camaro is just the same as his Lamborghini. When women pass a woman with "store-boughts" they look down their noses; when men pass the same woman they get that dreamy "Oooooh I'd love to take a nap or play a game of hubbledy bubbledy on that playground" look. Or just ask some random male how he feels about the subject and chances are better than even that he'd choose a matched, molded set. It also bears the implication that the male has enough money to buy them as a gift. I know that I was among the hundreds of thousands of women who missed that magic moment nearly fifty years ago. But it had profound meaning even for those who were there primarily for the music. After all, when Joan Baez endorsed our gathering, she meant it.

It was a great opportunity to gather enough atmosphere to carry us on to the next level of politics (when everybody had a theme song). It was also the moment for polished sorority sisters to shed their cardigans and knee socks along with their vassarettes.

Having solved the bra problem with beautiful lace, silk and no underwire at an authorized Jezebel dealer, we had resumed shopping for the unknown when my feet, wrapped in leather and "man-made materials uppers" suddenly seemed to catch fire. I kicked the offending articles off in the closest shoe store and sat down with my feet screaming for mercy. To add insult to injury was to realize that I was waaaaaayyy out of my allowance class. These were not cheap shoes. I got up from the chair and said to the ladies gathered there, "I would like to apologize to each of you individually and as representatives of your generation, for having spoken unkindly about my mother's sensible shoes." It appeared that my penance, which I welcomed, was to sit in that chair until I found a shoe that really fit. At last, nearly two and a half hours later, including time spent borrowing shoes from neighboring stores, I did indeed pick the ugliest shoe in the store, just my size, and I prayed for the perfect fit. And got it. And so it goes. I am only obliged to spread the good word, which I am doing with a passion. My clue is that my nieces and granddaughters hesitate a few seconds before accepting an invitation to go shopping with me these days. I know they are embarrassed by my shoe campaign, especially when I launch into the structural damage they are doing wearing five-inch platform heels. The fact that they are not required to register these shoes with the police department just like anyone else carrying a lethal weapon continues to boggle my mind.

Our very favorite contemporary fashion statement remains Those Pants and The Question everyone wants to have answered is "How Do Those Pants Stay Up???" It is this century's ponderable. So there I am, standing in a line behind one of the kids with his low slung pants hanging tenuously and I, for lack of other amusements, am openly studying them. You just know that with little or no encouragement, they'd be down around his ankles. Not having discovered anything new, I smiled benignly at the woman behind me. She smiled back with more than a hint of mischief and said only, "Give you a buck if you'll do it." I almost did. I think that the secret to Those Pants may be as simple as band aids and Velcro. I am also convinced that dressing outrageously is a perfect and conscious invitation to look. Being an obliging person by nature, I'd hate to send these fashion plates home unrequited. So I come to a full stop and simply stare until I have absorbed as much as I want, by which time my shopping companion has jumped ship and is waiting for me with enough lead time that no one would connect us easily.

So there you are: a shopping excursion to remember. One pair of unbelievably ugly shoes. A clearance shirt. The after-taste of stale pretzels with cheese. What could be more compelling? The favorite fashion statement is still Those Pants.

We all carry things in our cars that we hope never to use, like tire chains and first aid kits. We also have maps, but they find their way in nice little packets into the trunk. Obviously not high-use items. In fact, when asked about it, Catherine responded with, "When I was a kid, that's why you had the second seat. The person who sits there takes care of all that." (I'd love to know what planet she really comes from.) Your car must also carry everything you might need to change dinner plans, to clean up a spill, or to prove to the nice officer that you paid the parking tickets last spring and they are just temporarily lost in the console. One of the most important tools to have accessible in your glove compartment is a good pair of tweezers for those errant chin hairs that are only visible when you're in the car (in fact, you should carry a pair in your purse.) You must first get it through your head that no matter how attractive the guy in the classic fully restored Triumph TR3 happens to be, he's three lanes over and hasn't given you so much as a nod. The likelihood that he will suddenly whip over in your lane and blow kisses to you is zero. There is always the very remote chance that the gorgeous hunk on the freeway is headed for the same meeting you are, in which case you need a ready remark, something along the lines of "Nothing like a freshly polished chin to make you feel sharp." All of which is a long way to say, "Go ahead and tweeze to your heart's content." Go for it. We all know that a tweezed chin is important. You'll find that the half inch hair you couldn't leave alone during yesterday's meeting is gone. Without a trace. And now there's a curly one, completely invisible anywhere but the car. And we still have to worry about the etiquette: to tell or not to tell. I personally think that the rogue hair problem follows along the line with someone who comes out of a restroom with the hem of her skirt tucked into the waistband. Your options and decisions depend entirely on how much you like her and how much the wager is.

Hair has no limits when it comes to hair-related symptoms of aging. Or, just symptoms related to having hair. Of course there's gray hair, and the loss of body hair. Then you'll want to acknowledge the left-brain/right-brain theory that was so popular a couple of decades ago. Once you've taken that step, the rest just is. For example, people who are detail-oriented are likely to be left-brained; those who are creative are said to be right-brained. Now you can take notice: people turn gray more quickly on the side of the head they use most. It's true; check it out. Some people can even change their hair color by brushing it in the opposite direction than usual.

The most telling of our features are the lines people call Crows' Feet. Crows' Feet are among the most important features we have. These lines, radiating from the eye, reveal to even a casual observer your mood at that moment, your general temperament, and the depth of your sense of humor. They are not lines or wrinkles, as you might have thought. They are actually hairline cracks in the surface of the skin. Think of them much like the jagged cracks in the parched African tundra on your television every day and night thanks to National Geographic. What a forbidding sight! Why do they time the evisceration scenes to coincide with my dinner? Then, as if by magic, the rains come, and act just like EsteeLaudersuperduperskinrestorative available for only twice your current monthly salary or four times the amount of your allowance. When the humidity is a factor or when someone is trying to keep his or her thoughts in order, they look up in order to keep valuable thoughts from leaking out. Sometimes, a heavy thinker will even throw his or her head back and cover their eyes with an arm. These crevices are also sometimes charitably called "Smile Lines" or "Laugh Lines," in order to soften any comment that implies your face looks wadded up. It really is important to stay aware of Laugh Lines to keep them to a minimum. Likewise, too much time spent looking down can be disastrous to someone with a functioning brain. There is certainly the possibility that information worth retaining leaks out through the Crows' Feet.

19 Luggage and Margaritas

"Anybody want to go to Mexico??"

Well, good morning to you too, Monica. She certainly knows how to own the room. Even first thing in the morning. "When?" sez I. "Today," sez she. Well, you would have thought Hans Brinker had just pulled his finger out of the dam. Each of us had apparently been gathering trip information with Costa Rica in mind, forgetting completely that we had all agreed on San Miguel de Allende for our next trip. "We all still have current passports, plenty of food for snacking en route, a couple of changes of clothing." We all turn to check in with Alex, who wins the award for the greatest number of good questions asked and best use of a travel agent. She also looked a bit flushed, which could be the result of the sudden nature of the wake up call or it could be that there is truth to the story that Alex had taken a lover on her previous trip to San Miguel. At the idea of leaving spouses, we waffled a bit but decided that even one more person in the rental van would spell disaster or at least significant discomfort. And if we go to eight, it becomes a different trip entirely. So our patient spouses get cut from the herd again. Where do we stay? Do the houses generally have staff? Are there artists we want to take classes from? What do we know about restaurants there? "Call the travel agent," cried Catherine. Dead silence. "That would be us, Catherine," Monica reminded us. "We have no back up plan, kiddies. We're on our own. In other words, we're the grownups on this one." Sheer panic ruled for a few minutes and our pragmatist, Liz, stepped into the ring, looked at the five of us and said, "Is something preventing us from going to two places? Or even three?" Among Spanish-speaking destinations we've talked about are San Miguel de Allende and Cuernavaca. "Heaven forbid we should talk this trip to death like we did when it first came up," Monica reminded us. "Two years ago." There is no doubt that Rachel would go back to Costa Rica with its incredible jungles, waterfalls, ruins and rain forests in a heartbeat. She may never stop talking about the singing lizards, but even Rachel had to admit that the jungle isn't for everybody. Come to think of it, the only person I have ever met who looks right in a jungle is Rachel. Back to Alex with instructions to create an experience that would rival San Miguel de Allende in Cuernavaca, while we check each other's luggage for sufficiency and fix celebratory margaritas.

"Oh, for heaven's sake, I can be ready to go in an hour. We can do that, or we can dilly-dally on into next week or next month and never go anywhere." "Okay, I'm in," chimed Rachel. Amazing. Absolutely amazing. Everybody seemed to know what needed to be done and moved in the right directions. The marrieds called their spouses. Monica got the housekeeping staff corralled in the kitchen with Michael. One of the things threatening to drop right off our radar screen was the Grand Nuptials for Bert and Beverly. We had long ago identified the beginning of June for the wedding and we gave Michael his directions for that while we were gone. Bert did ask Michael to oversee any wedding planning, and we agreed that Beverly would step up to the plate in short order, especially when Michael nudged her a bit. Several tasks could be accomplished by computer (assuming we'd have internet). Things like invitations, gifts for the wedding party, music, furniture rentals, food and drink and enough of the right people to spread it around. And a honeymoon plan. From a public relations standpoint, this wedding was a showcase for our special events, so it needed to be a perfect ten on a scale of one to ten. And since the wedding was our gift to them, we didn't need any glitches, seen or unseen. I caught Bert before he left for work and he offered to use some of his billions of accumulated vacation and sick leave days and stay at the house. We suggested that he and Beverly spend some time planning the wedding and reviewed our calendars to see when we could close Madrigal for a couple of days. It still looked like the weekend of June first. And no, thank you, Beverly wouldn't stay at the house until after they were married. Wouldn't think of it.

Alex called her friend who had been to San Miguel de Allende several times on vacations good and bad. Alex was in clover planning a beauty event adventure for six people who are rarely critical. Rachel also called the Vice Principal of our favorite high school to let him know we'd be gone for almost ten days and would appreciate their just generally keeping an eye open. And we all felt confident that everybody was as ready as they could get. No reason to contact guests or anyone not on staff. So Monica, who started this, made the final move: she called a car to take us to the airport. We each had our latest rendition of computers with us, so we were not really planning a vacation of abandon, but pretty close. I've often thought that the perfect vacation would start with packing the clothes you feel like wearing, taking a car and driver to the airport and then, only then, do you study the departure boards and decide where you want to go. It should be noted that on this trip, the matched Samsonite didn't make the cut. But Alex noted for the record that this is not precedent setting. And I think I even saw a glimmer of a smile accompanying the announcement.

20 Happy As Clams At High Tide

I don't care where you put it, ninety-eight degrees is hot. Dry heat, wet heat. I'm not buying it. With steam rising from the cobblestones, you can bet it's hot. The pressure on Alex to have made the right arrangements was overwhelming. But she had all the luck in Mexico on her side, starting with tall, handsome Alejo, who was charged with getting the six of us and our luggage from the plane, into the van and to our casa. We apparently missed the afternoon rain shower, but everything looked freshly washed so we didn't miss it by much. Our gate opened onto a cobblestone courtyard with a profusion of colors set in unbelievably lush native greenery, seating for eight and wonderful, whimsical pottery and art. Alejo, who did speak a little English, gestured us to the seats and said he would return shortly. And return he did, with Señora Escobar, the effusive owner of the house who lives with her husband in a separate casita on the property. She is dark and imposing. Her skin is beautiful, but that's because it's full. Sra. Escobar immediately engaged us in a timeworn and well-choreographed welcoming dance and let us know that she is Yoli to us. She introduced the cook, Victoria, the maid, and another general helper whose name escaped me immediately. "Please," Yoli said in flawless colloquial English, "make this your home here. You are welcome to entertain, to treat staff as if they were your own. Feel free to keep them from being bored. And be sure to let the kitchen help perform. We just stole Victoria from one of the best restaurants in the region." In another sleight of hand maneuver, Yoli produced a fist-full of brochures touting the art of San Miguel – where to learn it and where to buy it – and some cooking classes we might not want to miss. "But where are my manners?" Yoli exclaimed. "I must have left them in Guadalajara! Come, come. Let's show you the rest of your casa!"

Six bedrooms, each with full bath, two family rooms with entertainment centers, (audio in English) and exquisite art everywhere you looked. Alex gets a free pass for hooking us up with Yoli. We could only hope that Alex would do half as well with the second assignment as she did with San Miguel. And so she did. A southern California transplant with a fairy tale "second home" in Cuernavaca occasionally rents his incredibly beautiful castillo to trusted dignitaries, friends and relatives for a comparatively paltry sum, or else there was a superb hotel, Las Mañanitas, which offered rival but different delights. Ideally, we'd like to spend Friday through Thursday in San Miguel de Allende and Thursday until Sunday in Cuernavaca.

As a welcoming gift to us, Yoli had arranged to have a mariachi group perform in our courtyard for a couple of hours while we dined on the most pluperfect buffet featuring local dishes prepared by Victoria, who enjoyed showing off to a new group. Yoli explained that many houses in this particular neighborhood are occupied by Americans, and what better way to get to know them? It was all very congenial, but by ten o'clock we were ready for sleep. Happy as clams at high tide.

Up at the crack of late morning we started right out filling our faces with huevos rancheros, corn and hominy soufflé, refried beans, fresh tortillas cooked on the grill while we ate, papaya, and freshly baked bread. Among other things, traveling in late April or early May gives you the most powerful show of flowers everywhere you look. The greens are deep and rich, and the colors of the flowers are breathtaking. We counted no fewer than thirty-nine shades of green in one courtyard alone and revised our agenda to start with buying a couple of reference books to enable us to not look completely ignorant on our walking tour. Not that I had ever in my entire life been able to actually find a bird or a plant in a bird or plant book, but hope springs eternal. Almost.

First, we inadvertently, and literally, fell into an art school when Alex turned her ankle straining to check the price on a magnificent Talavera-style bowl. She refused assistance for the first stretch of the walk and then capitulated in favor of not worsening the sprain. Liz was out of her orthopedic accessories, so we had plenty of equipment for protecting such injuries. All left at Madrigal. Having been given directions to a local farmacia, we soon had Alex suitably bandaged in an elegant ankle-support that somehow lent an extra queenly measure to her step.

Yoli may have alerted us to this weekend's activity, but if so, in our fatigue and excitement, it slipped through the cracks. But it didn't take us long to figure out that we were smack dab in the middle of a nationally promoted annual festival: La Fiesta de Las Flores. Residents shine up their courtyards and open the gates for all to see. Some even set out light refreshments. In the face of such hospitality, how could you refuse the tapas no matter how unlike American food they looked?

Happily, we headed for "our" casa and lunch and an undisturbed siesta, from which we arose refreshed, energized and ready to party. San Miguel is the very best place to feel that way. Locals put themselves out for visitors and make everyone feel valued. Which, in fact, we are, since we're the buyers (at whatever scale). A young American woman living in San Miguel recounted her first weeks in San Miguel as a fantasyland for shoppers. Her parents would hand her a fistful of money and send her off to "shop." She could amuse herself for an entire day on fifty cents, trading, buying, learning Spanish and sometimes making a tidy profit acting as an agent for tourists. (Of course this is the young woman who staged a yard sale when her parents were out of town.)

Because of the Fiesta everything was open late and we wandered into a courtyard gallery where the artist was holding court. Her style was reminiscent of a young Frida Kahlo, without the macabre themes, and she happened to be promoting her classes. What a find! Catherine, Alex and Monica signed up immediately, made nice-nice with the artist and promised to be there at precisely nine thirty, right after breakfast, not knowing, of course, that "precisely" has no equivalent in the Mexican language. Liz, Rachel and I decided to wander on foot, stopping wherever our curiosity took us. For some reason, we felt no pressure to shop, despite the fact that we had brought pretty much nothing more than a change in underwear. Catherine observed that when surrounded by such beauty you just blend in. I'm not sure I buy it, but I certainly like it. Monica, spotting a remarkable outfit, as is her style, went straight to the source, asking the very attractive woman where she got her sensational dress. The lady responded cheerily, "Nordstrom's. They carry all the classic Josefa designs." You can imagine the conversation! Funny we had to travel all those miles to find Mexican designer clothing.

Creatures of habit that we are, we kept coming back to the subject of food as if we were about to starve. Is anybody hungry? Not possible. We consumed the equivalent of at least one full meal during our meanderings. Should we make dinner reservations? Will staff still be there when we get back to the casa? Talk about unnecessary worry, religiously reminding ourselves to "save room" for what "our" staff might be preparing. And were they ever!!

By the time we met back at the house, we were some combination of exhausted, excited, overwhelmed, and ready for more. Can you be overcome by beauty overload? If it's possible, just load us into the back of a flatbed truck and haul us away.

Monica, whose collection of silver jewelry is quite covetable, couldn't seem to stop thinking about a couple of pieces she had seen on her stroll through San Miguel. One is a wide hinged cuff wrapped twice intertwined with grapes about the size of small champagne grapes. She resisted buying it by picking up a few things for her kids and a small dresser dish with Mayan symbols around the perimeter. But the bracelet was still there. And we still had plenty of time and energy to visit them tomorrow. As for the other piece she was trying to resist, it defies sober description. Suffice to say the primary elements are silver, pearls, opals and just a hint of rubies. As we had walked home up the slick little cobblestone street earlier, Rachel asked if anyone knew how far we'd walked that day. Don't know. Don't care. I know we walked far enough that my legs were ready to lie down. This is NOT a competitive event, Rachel.

21 Ramifications

Six seems to be the perfect number for a group like ours. It leaves enough space for disagreement and even for taking sides. If in a restaurant, cafe or bar, we carry enough volume in our conversations that we can clear the room, intimidating any wimpy little servers into painful obsequiousness.

We were still sliding down the backside of the valium-laced 1950s, finding things to occupy our minds and bodies without rattling our mothers. There is practically no limit to the things you can make using discarded goods left meaningfully on the floor of the den and one guest room. Advertising of the day showed us adorable little girls in pinafores and aprons sitting on tall stools, listening to every word, learning to cook. An ashtray might be on the counter, along with a glass of something tasty and refreshing. Often sporting a lime wedge. We were the first generation to be invited to smoke cigarettes, even if only second hand. They had to get us. They had to get us because we weren't paying attention. Why else would Dorothy Kilgallen's name mean anything to me? And our own mothers gave us up to those purveyors of mind-numbing games televised each afternoon. From secret high cupboards, they took yards of uncut fabrics from an almost uncut bolt of olive drab corduroy and little bitty calico prints and taught us how to make Ginny doll dresses for other victims of Filling Leisure Time. And now, there we were at an indoor/outdoor mosaic class. $40. Basically killing time in a socially acceptable manner. The crafts teacher immediately started with a sales pitch to get us to buy a birdbath or a reflecting ball. As politely as possible, I explained that I had no need or desire for birdbaths and the like. Liz agreed. We went back and forth for several minutes until Liz put an end to it with a very carefully enunciated, "I do not want a birdbath. I just want to know how it's done." "Oh," she says, still missing the point altogether. "What do you want to put into the garden?" Nothing. Nada. Zip. In my world, no is a complete sentence. How about if you just bring me a rock to decorate? So Liz and I retired to the glass breaking part of the project, finishing it easily without becoming pests.

When all of the ironing has been done and the dinner is well on its way to completion, then, and only then, can we bring out The Box of craft treasures and apply ourselves to the creation of Christmas for the best friends. Even though this is May. You can't get started early enough for the treasured personalized jelly jar covers, the loom crocheted pot-holders or my runaway favorite: the crocheted toilet paper holder. Can you imagine a home without one? Or two?

It's not hard to picture the contents of The Box. Beads and rhinestones, arranged by size and then color, buttons, pieces of ribbon, felt squares, several colors of embroidery thread, five or six quilt squares but no evidence of further effort or interest, and a few skeins of yarn provide all of the entertainment anyone could need or want. But no. Not the truly industrious ones. They first find the library and then set about learning everything to know about flowers, then small animals, and then birds. They could identify a bullet hawk from a mile away, and then pass the information to their ever knowledgeable husbands, whose reputation for wildlife facts and fiction remains unparalleled and unchallenged.

Some people, I'm afraid, should not undertake crafts of any kind, especially the fine arts. Those with no facility for painting or sculpture are not likely to develop it out of the clear blue in their sixties. But there are exceptions. People who have suffered with repressed talent can be a bit troublesome and there may be insufficient praise in the universe to sustain these late-comers. The first crafts class that comes to mind is the most recent one: a spin at pastels. Catherine, who really is artistic, produced a lovely still life in her first foray into pastels, followed by some florals and some sky-scapes. I took the seaside sunset route and delivered a thoroughly dull gray piece of paper lacking only the tire treads for cultural accuracy. Now we know why they touch you lightly and say "Pastels are soooooo forgiving." Our instructor had the courtesy to make her comments about my work brief and generic. I do believe that I don't have to go in that direction again.

One might ask where these urges to dabble into crafts come from…and where they go when we move on to something slightly more adult. One day we're decorating cigar boxes with scandalous découpage nudes, the next arranging flowers for an event at the club.

Summers, of course, provided other pursuits. Boys. Not boys soon to be young men. Boys named Doug and Russell who would simply love to take advantage of these girls with their budding breasts, figures and rudimentary flirting skills. But they're chicken. Just plain chicken. The third leg of this learning triangle is mother. Mother voted with the kids in favor of spending the vacation money on three weeks of summer vacation rental at the beach, only to remember (too late) that the beach is one huge job with little or no recompense, especially when you add in the preservation of mid-adolescent virtue. And as for the virtue element, I cannot imagine how anyone gets a handle on a bunch of boys who will cover for each other instinctively and share their finds, starting at birth. I can see now where I went wrong as a babysitter. Rather than bury these babies in toys and stuff, gently place their hands near each other's equipment and you've given them a life of discovery. Girls, however, can't even manage to keep quiet while looking for the concrete block that was placed crooked apparently primarily for viewing purposes. And the minute they get silly, the boys take off for parts unknown. How very little changes as the boys get older.

As was generally the case during the summer months, the kids were subject to the various disciplinary whims and everybody's kids were fair game for all the adults. The way the club was laid out, the road down the hill from the houses was quite steep but also quite direct. You could drive down to the beach, in which case you would stop at the adult refreshment stand (an ice chest) and talk endlessly about the six foot stingaree (aka "sting ray"). It scared the younger kids half to death, but if you could get maybe half a dozen kids out of the water, it made for much better fishing and surfing (my dad was, of course, a sensational body surfer and fisherman). The next stop was the volleyball court, where we stopped long enough to absorb all of the pertinent info about any possible interlopers. Then, not before we had unloaded the car and set up camp, the kids exploded with beach energy (harder to get, but also harder to slough off.) We had gym equipment and horseshoes, many had small boats and always a drop dead handsome lifeguard. And, my favorite: diatomatious earth. There's always a spoiled brat that uses smarts to ride roughshod over their peers and in this case it was me truly who went straight home to the encyclopedia and learned all kinds of extraneous nonsense. Because I was so snotty about it, that information will stay with me forever. So if anybody asks you about it, demur gently.

It is only fair to note that that particular Saturday, the one that we all recall so vividly, had other reasons for fame. Stephanie and her three goody goody sons arrived at the beach at about 1:00. Stephanie was, in the opinion of all us kids, the most snooty member in the whole club. In a simultaneous but unrelated moment, Stephanie, a full-time resident, let her beautiful dog, an Afghan named Chim, out on the sand. As we all expected, Stephanie simply held her ground when Chim came sniffing around, ostensibly to get acquainted with Boss, a big, loveable mastiff from further down the beach. The two giant dogs romping around on the sand went a long way toward reducing the numbers of swimmers and sunbathers. But, wherever dogs are, they still have business to take care of. You can see it happen. One minute they're sniffing that inquiry sniff and a second later, it's the, "Hey, buddy, you mind closing the door?" Sure enough, Chim spied a likely target, circled deliberately behind the beach chair, turned up on Stephanie and continued on his way down the beach. Game over. I understood the word "ramifications" and that Chim had plenty of them. And I was at least ten when I learned that those hang-y down things were not really called ramifications.

22 A State Of Perpetual Road Repair

Just as we were getting comfortable with San Miguel de Allende's streets and activities, mostly focused on food and fabulous art, the tardy bell sounded a reminder that we wanted to get to Cuernavaca before dark and before they gave away our dinner reservations or our room. We snuggled into the rental van and knew we'd be back.

There was no doubt that we had planned too much in too little time, but how are you going to see the world otherwise? We hopped into the van, ready for anything. Almost. Small hiccup: Rachel is a firm believer that you only have to be traveling a little bit slower than the driver next to you. And it's good if you arrive at your destination at the same time your car does.

We were only slightly slowed down by clumps of dusty men, ostensibly repairing the road. Government inspection and highway workers notwithstanding, the paved roads in Mexico are like that chocolate sundae topping that solidifies on contact with ice-cream. Suddenly we found ourselves moving not forwards but downwards, as a huge sink hole opened under the front wheels of our big rental van. We were decidedly in peril. We and our possessions were headed for the slippery slopes below with nothing to grab onto but each other. When any one of us shifted weight, the van produced that grinding sound that presages doom in disaster movies. What to do? Nothing but to climb out of the van with the help of one of the highway workers, and step over the microscopic guardrail. Our gallant savior then rounded up a band of his compadres who, with extraordinary cheerfulness and many shouted instructions one to another, quite literally manhandled the van out of the sink hole and deposited it safely on the other side. Gingerly, we skirted around the perfectly circular abyss, encouraged and occasionally supported by our band of rescuers, until we too stood solidly on the other side, reunited with our vehicle and everything it held. With many heartfelt "thank yous" and protestations of undying obligation (on our side) and devotion (on theirs), we parted company and set off once more.

Soon we arrived in Cuernavaca.

Gone the colors of San Miguel, so full and rich that they seem to shimmer, which is probably sunlight filtered through the raindrops, so colorful as to be nearly violent. Cuernavaca is a bit more serene. Not subdued, not modest, certainly not tailored; bougainvillea cascades over every wall in more colors than we were prepared for. It's no wonder that it is known as the Garden City of Mexico. Furthermore, Cuernavaca will always have the distinction of being the city in which Alex was awarded the First Madrigal Splendor Award given for excellence in planning and delivering a trip to beat all expectations. Thanks to Alex's skillful efforts in route planning and destination recognition we arrived at Las Mañanitas, a magnificent five-star inn that was once a private residence owned by a Mexican actor of note turned corporate mogul. We pulled in just in time to get one of the two superb upstairs suites, extravagantly appointed for six. When you arrive downstairs, you are shown to your cocktail table, which is discreetly situated next to the pond or some other beautiful spot on the acres of manicured grounds. While your dinner table is being set, you have still more appetizers or a plate of crab fries. Our hors d'oeuvres plates were never empty and we were never aware of staff hovering nearby. We were first served a tureen of fresh vegetable bisque, followed by an assortment of fresh marinated langostinos, rich and extremely delicate, followed by perfectly prepared side dishes, and desserts fit for royalty. The description is inadequate by miles, but you get the picture. And then, sisters, they bring on course after course of the most delectable local foods. The leisurely dinner wasn't even prohibitive. I'm sure we've paid more at home for a dramatically lesser meal. Makes me wonder if you can't buy a plot. Here you go, Monica.

The next day our thoughts turned insistently toward Madrigal and the impending wedding. We knew without a smidgen of doubt that at that hour the four of them – Bert, Beverly and Trudy, the Maid of Honor, and Michael – were clustered in the library trying to convince Beverly that being generous gives Bert great pleasure. As you might guess, her first choice for the wedding dress was a nice turquoise knee length shirtdress she bought for a friend's wedding five years before. She got ZERO support on that one. She explained that she wanted no attendants because she had no family to give her away. Huh? Try again, Beverly.

We decided to Skype them because this is worth an hour and a half of nitpicking. We found they had several things resolved, like the graceful two-piece wedding suit in ecru silk shantung. Fortunately, Beverly is a perfect size eight.

They fully expected to hit a snag when they opened the subject of where to live together and were delighted that the decision had been made: they would live in Beverly's house for several reasons, not the least of which is that her house is cleaner. As for the honeymoon, they both chose an Alaskan cruise from which they could hook up with the elite, luxurious Lewis & Clark excursions. Travelers by nature, both bride and groom loved the concept of not going anywhere either of them had visited before. As Beverly said, travelling that way makes life seem so boundless…and every day so new. I can't promise I'd feel that way if I was travelling with a grouch, but I'd try.

Music, on the other hand, foretold no landmines until Michael assumed aloud that Billy Jack was the music director. First things first: was he available for the wedding? Did he have any desire to assume that role? Even on the phone his enthusiasm was palpable. And would we like to have him come by in a few minutes to audition? Michael explained that the six ladies were in Mexico on vacation, but Bert, Beverly and Michael had the authority to make those kinds of decisions and yes, they would like to have him come by, the sooner the better.

He must have flown. After three beautiful classic pieces (processional, Bride's song and the recessional) played flawlessly by Billy Jack's trio, the mood was set. At each table we would have a black-tied student server to ensure that all guests are happy and satisfied. They have also ordered a large dance floor expecting it to match the music selection. Just remember the variety of music we feasted on in the sixties and you'll know how much fun there was to be had, no question about it. We got Percy Faith back to back with Creedence Clearwater Revival and Aretha Franklin as lead-ins to Frank Sinatra, immediately following The Who. Indeed, music would make the day. Each table would have a music menu and anyone thinking that the Guest List is easier than the Music Menu is nuts.

The process of developing a credible music list crosses all socio-economic lines but in the end, the right people seem to surface. But the guest list - aaaaahhh. The dreaded Guest List. How does anyone figure out who goes on The List anyway? Seems to me that the Wedding Guest List must include:

1. Immediate family not in prison
2. Immediate family in public office (may overlap with #1)
3. Anyone you know with two commas in their monthly take-home income
4. All people living within three blocks of the house or the church where the reception will be held
5. All family members on the Family Tree down to second cousins twice removed
6. Co-workers, social friends and acquaintances

We ended the Skype call with (moderate) confidence that all was well in hand.

23 Applause, Tears, Laughter, Cheers...

We all know that Monica purchases her exquisite silver pieces mostly in New Mexico, but Taxco is a more-than-worthy alternative and many of the silversmiths and artists there exhibit at international museums of note, attaining fame well beyond the borders, so we set off, not telling Monica our destination, as it was to be a birthday surprise.

When our rented VW van gave up the ghost on a hardscrabble piece of earth midway between Cuernavaca and Taxco, we opted to hang in for the ride. Logic was on our side. There was, after all, a fenced corral for the rancher's goats, a darling pup, a yearling calf and tantalizingly, a mercado, which was horribly unrelated to VONS. Small flaw: there was no water to be found. And no melon in the field adjacent to the little "yard." It is also interesting to note that eight of every ten cars that drove past us sported Texas license plates and showed no inclination to offer help. I called Hertz every half hour to check on the status of our rental car. They finally got us a replacement at 7:00. Not happy.

We could have driven right past Taxco because Monica didn't have a clue...until she stepped out of the car and a brand new source of silver took her breath away. Taxco is a tiny town, a grotto carved out of a mountainside with veins of silver. Many of the world's finest, most creative artists descend upon Taxco in the last two weeks of May to celebrate and pay homage to the gods and the goddesses of silver and art and the glory they are together. Only Liz and I knew going in that the special pieces created for the Festival are available for purchase and that Monica's husband had given us a hunk of cash to buy her an anniversary gift. Then when she fell in love with the incredible piece in San Miguel de Allende, visiting it daily, we had a quandary on our hands. Buy according to the husband's insufficient knowledge or buy one of the Taxco festival necklaces, which can never be duplicated and are as sensual as can be. We mulled, we debated, we pondered, we mused, we whined. We did everything we could, missing the guy with the bankroll. What else could we do but call the guy whose idea it was. Besides which, we didn't really have time for an easy meander 'tween here and there. I was already nervous about going through customs with all our loot. Monica's husband was unequivocal in his instructions: go for the sensuous splendor of the Taxco piece. Accordingly, Liz slipped unobtrusively away and made the purchase, secreting the piece on her person until such time that she could hand it over to Ted who would then present it, with appropriate ceremony, to the astonished Monica.

The trip home was thoroughly uneventful, just as it should be. And there is a benefit in leaving your property with people who know you well. And who want to please you. When we walked in the door, there was a palpable lack of the ease we'd gotten accustomed to. Michael was mysteriously absent (we learned later that he had gone to make the final arrangements for the hire of the wedding carriage). Dorothy tried to account for his absence, but as Bert was present, she could not give the true reason and, unaccustomed to subterfuge, choked on her carefully prepared speech. Baffled at the time, we were soon reassured by whispered conversations in corners.

Part of Bert's indefatigable charm is that he somehow

is able to evade all things sinister, always emerging from iffy activities smelling like the proverbial rose. As such, he was also uncomfortable with the entire genre of humor-laden practical jokes.

Enter Socorro, whose diminutive size and manner made her the perfect foil for the unexpected. She was known to pop out of a lower kitchen cabinet and politely say "Boo" just because she could. Or deliver a bogus message to a favored guest.

But, lo and behold, as Angel related to us with giggly relish, the prankster extraordinaire turned out to be Beverly, with Socorro a tiger in the backup position. Knowing full well that Bert knew nothing about computers, Beverly, who worked at the Apple store, had decided to make our Skype call an occasion for some hilarity. After dinner, on cue, Beverly asked Bert to bring in the laptop, which he carried like the bones of a revered deceased relative. He heard a little squeak from the machine and immediately reported its appearance. The computer made another little wounded mouse sound and Bert froze. As the laptop made yet another little noise, Beverly said, looking very much like the classic deer in the headlights, "Oh, dear, Socorro, you don't suppose it could be one of those roach infestations, do you?" Our groom, who was by now nearly comatose with terror, choked and said hopefully but with trepidation, "This isn't one of those TV shows, is it?" He was firmly convinced it was and remains so to this day.

Everyone has a favorite slice of the Wedding. As you might guess, people with financial interests in matrimonia seem more alert to revenue centers. Pretty girls who strive to beauty are inordinately fascinated by the bridesmaids and their finery. Musical aficionados will aver that the only good part of a wedding is the recessional: that sunny ditty announcing the union of the happy couple. Whatever your choice, this wedding had it in spades. We had canapés to beat the band, followed by two hundred exquisite dinners served, non-stop dancing, a championship bocce ball tournament in progress. It wasn't as if the bocce ball game usurped the players' interest. It's just that it was the second to final match and we needed all the talent we could muster. And there were plenty of mimosas.

Just as the magnificent cake was to be brought to its table, a wedding carriage bedecked with hundreds of flowers came up through the bocce court carrying the nine-tier confectioner's masterpiece. Applause, tears, laughter, cheers…it was all there and, in a flash of a big old-fashioned camera, they had left.

Once all was quiet and no guests remained, we gathered, the six of us, on the porch. Liz passed round the boxes of photos, and together we laughed and cried over all they brought to mind.

The next generation of us is already out there vowing not to let a house run their lives. Soon enough, they'll figure out that The Dream is theirs for the asking. Next time we'll be kinder to our significant others.

Acknowledgments

To the sisters of TTT, who have provided inspiration in their every move. They represent, individually and collectively, all that women can be. And are certainly not ordinary.

To Sarah Williams, Managing Director at The Book Consultancy, who has always been enthusiastic in her support in having this story told. Full of humor and sensitivity, she brings her talents for all to share.

To Charles and Kristen Utts, who are enthusiastic and creative production partners and friends.

To Alice, who was there supporting this book with love, care and generosity from the first step to the last.

To all those who provided input and support all along the way, especially Lynn, a wonderful friend and ally.

About The Author

Teresa Raley is a remarkable, insightful woman with diverse talents who believes that nothing is impossible if you have enough conviction to just get busy and do it.

She is a partner in a public relations, advertising and graphic design firm with her husband. In addition to writing, she excels at open mosaic glasswork and construction of architectural miniatures in several media. She is a trusted and respected member of her business community, and is a sensitive, devoted, loving friend, daughter, mother, grandmother, and wife.

This is her first novel.
She, her husband and their black Labrador Retriever live in Southern California.